THE GLENCOE LITERATURE LIBRARY

# Julie
## of the
# Wolves

**and Related Readings**

Glencoe
McGraw-Hill

New York, New York   Columbus, Ohio   Woodland Hills, California   Peoria, Illinois

## Acknowledgments

Grateful acknowledgment is given authors, publishers, photographers, museums, and agents for permission to reprint the following copyrighted material. Every effort has been made to determine copyright owners. In case of any omissions, the Publisher will be pleased to make suitable acknowledgments in future editions.

JULIE OF THE WOLVES by Jean Craighead George. Copyright © 1972 by Jean Craighead George. Used by permission of HarperCollins Publishers.

"The Wolves" excerpted from JEAN CRAIGHEAD GEORGE by Alice Cary. Copyright © 1996 by The Learning Works, Inc., Santa Barbara, CA. Reprinted by permission.

Text excerpt "Killing to Survive" from WOLF PACK: TRACKING WOLVES IN THE WILD by Sylvia A. Johnson and Alice Aamodt. Copyright © 1985 Lerner Publications Company. Reprinted by permission of Lerner Publications Co., Minneapolis, MN.

Text excerpt from JULIE'S WOLF PACK by Jean Craighead George. Text copyright © 1997 by Jean Craighead George. Used by permission of HarperCollins Publishers.

Excerpted from CELEBRATE THE STATES: ALASKA by Rebecca Stefoff. Copyright © 1998 Benchmark Books, Marshall Cavendish Corp. Reprinted by permission of the publisher.

Text excerpt "Two Inches Above the Television Screen" pp. 6–10 and Notes p. 101 from LIFE IN AN ESKIMO VILLAGE by Gail B. Stewart, Lucent Books. Reprinted by permission of Lucent Books.

Excerpts from THE IGLOO. Copyright © 1988 by Charlotte Yue and David Yue. Reprinted by permission of Houghton Mifflin Company. All rights reserved.

**Cover Art**: Courtesy of Wild Wings, Inc., Lake City, MN 55041

*Glencoe/McGraw-Hill*

*A Division of The **McGraw·Hill** Companies*

Send all inquiries to:
**Glencoe/McGraw-Hill**
8787 Orion Place
Columbus, OH 43240

ISBN 0-02-817998-6
Printed in the United States of America
2 3 4 5 6 7 8 9 026 04 03 02 01 00

# Contents

## Julie of the Wolves

## Related Readings

# Julie
## of the
# Wolves

**Jean Craighead George**

# Part I

# Amaroq, the Wolf

**M**IYAX PUSHED BACK the hood of her sealskin parka and looked at the Arctic sun. It was a yellow disc in a lime-green sky, the colors of six o'clock in the evening and the time when the wolves awoke. Quietly she put down her cooking pot and crept to the top of a dome-shaped frost heave, one of the many earth buckles that rise and fall in the crackling cold of the Arctic winter. Lying on her stomach, she looked across a vast lawn of grass and moss and focused her attention on the wolves she had come upon two sleeps ago. They were wagging their tails as they awoke and saw each other.

Her hands trembled and her heartbeat quickened, for she was frightened, not so much of the wolves, who were shy and many harpoon-shots away, but because of her desperate predicament. Miyax was lost. She had been lost without food for many sleeps on the North Slope of Alaska. The barren slope stretches for two hundred miles from the Brooks Range to the Arctic Ocean, and for more than eight hundred miles from Canada to the Chukchi Sea. No roads cross it; ponds and lakes freckle its immensity. Winds scream across it, and the view in every direction is exactly the same. Somewhere in this cosmos was Miyax; and the very life in her body, its spark and warmth, depended upon these wolves for survival. And she was not so sure they would help.

Miyax stared hard at the regal black wolf, hoping to catch his eye. She must somehow tell him that she was starving and ask him for food. This could be done she knew, for her father, an Eskimo hunter, had done so. One year he had camped near a wolf den while on a hunt. When a month had passed and her father had seen no game, he told the leader of the wolves that he was hungry and needed food. The next night the wolf called him from far away and her father went to him and found a freshly killed caribou. Unfortunately, Miyax's father never explained to her how he had told the wolf of his needs.

And not long afterward he paddled his kayak into the Bering Sea to hunt for seal, and he never returned.

She had been watching the wolves for two days, trying to discern which of their sounds and movements expressed goodwill and friendship. Most animals had such signals. The little Arctic ground squirrels flicked their tails sideways to notify others of their kind that they were friendly. By imitating this signal with her forefinger, Miyax had lured many a squirrel to her hand. If she could discover such a gesture for the wolves she would be able to make friends with them and share their food, like a bird or a fox.

Propped on her elbows with her chin in her fists, she stared at the black wolf, trying to catch his eye. She had chosen him because he was  much larger than the others, and because he walked like her father, Kapugen, with his head high and his chest out. The black wolf also possessed wisdom, she had observed. The pack looked to him when the wind carried strange scents or the birds cried nervously. If he was alarmed, they were alarmed. If he was calm, they were calm.

Long minutes passed, and the black wolf did not look at her. He had ignored her since she first came upon them, two sleeps ago. True, she moved slowly and quietly, so as not to alarm him; yet she did wish he would see the kindness in her eyes. Many animals could tell the difference between hostile hunters and friendly people by merely looking at them. But the big black wolf would not even glance her way.

A bird stretched in the grass. The wolf looked at it. A flower twisted in the wind. He glanced at that. Then the breeze rippled the wolverine ruff on Miyax's parka and it glistened in the light. He did not look at that. She waited. Patience with the ways of nature had been instilled in her by her father. And so she knew better than to move or shout. Yet she must get food or die. Her hands shook slightly and she swallowed hard to keep calm.

Miyax was a classic Eskimo beauty, small of bone and delicately wired with strong muscles. Her face was pearl-round and her nose was flat. Her black eyes, which slanted gracefully, were moist and sparkling. Like the beautifully formed polar bears and foxes of the north, she was slightly short-limbed. The frigid environment of the Arctic has sculptured life into compact shapes. Unlike the long-limbed, long-bodied animals of the south that are cooled by dispensing heat on extended surfaces, all live things in the Arctic tend toward compactness, to conserve heat.

The length of her limbs and the beauty of her face were of no use to Miyax as she lay on the lichen-speckled frost heave in the midst of the bleak tundra. Her stomach ached and the royal black wolf was carefully ignoring her.

"Amaroq, ilaya, wolf, my friend," she finally called. "Look at me. Look at me."

She spoke half in Eskimo and half in English, as if the instincts of her father and the science of the gussaks, the white-faced, might evoke some magical combination that would help her get her message through to the wolf.

Amaroq glanced at his paw and slowly turned his head her way without lifting his eyes. He licked his shoulder. A few matted hairs sprang apart and twinkled individually. Then his eyes sped to each of the three adult wolves that made up his pack and finally to the five pups who were sleeping in a fuzzy mass near the den entrance. The great wolf's eyes softened at the sight of the little wolves, then quickly hardened into brittle yellow jewels as he scanned the flat tundra.

Not a tree grew anywhere to break the monotony of the gold-green plain, for the soils of the tundra are permanently frozen. Only moss, grass, lichens, and a few hardy flowers take root in the thin upper layer that thaws briefly in summer. Nor do many species of animals live in this rigorous land, but those creatures that do dwell here exist in bountiful numbers. Amaroq watched a large cloud of Lapland longspurs wheel up into the sky, then alight in the grasses. Swarms of crane flies, one of the few insects that can survive the cold, darkened the tips of the mosses. Birds wheeled, turned, and called. Thousands sprang up from the ground like leaves in a wind.

The wolf's ears cupped forward and turned in on some distant message from the tundra. Miyax tensed and listened, too. Did he hear some brewing storm, some approaching enemy? Apparently not. His ears relaxed and he rolled to his side. She sighed, glanced at the vaulting sky, and was painfully aware of her predicament.

Here she was, watching wolves—she, Miyax, daughter of Kapugen, adopted child of Martha, citizen of the United States, pupil at the Bureau of Indian Affairs School in Barrow, Alaska, and thirteen-year-old wife of the boy Daniel. She shivered at the thought of Daniel, for it was he who had driven her to this fate. She had run away from him exactly seven sleeps ago, and because of this she had one more title by gussak standards—the child divorcée.

The wolf rolled to his belly.

"Amaroq," she whispered. "I am lost and the sun will not set for a month. There is no North Star to guide me."

Amoroq did not stir.

"And there are no berry bushes here to bend under the polar wind and point to the south. Nor are there any birds I can follow." She looked up. "Here the birds are buntings and longspurs. They do not fly to the sea twice a day like the puffins and sandpipers that my father followed."

The wolf groomed his chest with his tongue.

"I never dreamed I could get lost, Amoroq," she went on, talking out loud to ease her fear. "At home on Nunivak Island where I was born, the plants and birds pointed the way for wanderers. I thought they did so everywhere . . . and so, great black Amoroq, I'm without a compass."

It had been a frightening moment when two days ago she realized that the tundra was an ocean of grass on which she was circling around and around. Now as that fear overcame her again she closed her eyes. When she opened them her heart skipped excitedly. Amoroq was looking at her!

"Ee-lie," she called and scrambled to her feet. The wolf arched his neck and narrowed his eyes. He pressed his ears forward. She waved. He drew back his lips and showed his teeth. Frightened by what seemed a snarl, she lay down again. When she was flat on her stomach, Amoroq flattened his ears and wagged his tail once. Then he tossed his head and looked away.

Discouraged, she wriggled backward down the frost heave and arrived at her camp feet first. The heave was between herself and the wolf pack and so she relaxed, stood up, and took stock of her home. It was a simple affair, for she had not been able to carry much when she ran away; she took just those things she would need for the journey—a backpack, food for a week or so, needles to mend clothes, matches, her sleeping skin, and ground cloth to go under it, two knives, and a pot.

She had intended to walk to Point Hope. There she would meet the *North Star*, the ship that brings supplies from the States to the towns on the Arctic Ocean in August when the ice pack breaks up. The ship could always use dishwashers or laundresses, she had heard, and so she would work her way to San Francisco where Amy, her pen pal, lived. At the end of every letter Amy always wrote: "When are you coming to San Francisco?" Seven days ago she had been on her

**4**     JULIE OF THE WOLVES

way—on her way to the glittering, white, postcard city that sat on a hill among trees, those enormous plants she had never seen. She had been on her way to see the television and carpeting in Amy's school, the glass buildings, traffic lights, and stores full of fruits; on her way to the harbor that never froze and the Golden Gate Bridge. But primarily she was on her way to be rid of Daniel, her terrifying husband.

She kicked the sod at the thought of her marriage; then shaking her head to forget, she surveyed her camp. It was nice. Upon discovering the wolves, she had settled down to live near them in the hope of sharing their food, until the sun set and the stars came out to guide her. She had built a house of sod, like the summer homes of the old Eskimos. Each brick had been cut with her ulo, the half-moon shaped woman's knife, so versatile it can trim a baby's hair, slice a tough bear, or chip an iceberg.

Her house was not well built for she had never made one before, but it was cozy inside. She had windproofed it by sealing the sod bricks with mud from the pond at her door, and she had made it beautiful by spreading her caribou ground cloth on the floor. On this she had spread her sleeping skin, a moosehide bag lined with soft white rabbit skins. Next to her bed she had built a low table of sod on which to put her clothes when she slept. To decorate the house she had made three flowers of bird feathers and stuck them in the top of the table. Then she had built a fireplace outdoors and placed her pot beside it. The pot was empty, for she had not found even a lemming to eat.

Last winter, when she had walked to school in Barrow, these mice-like rodents were so numerous they ran out from under her feet wherever she stepped. There were thousands and thousands of them until December, when they suddenly vanished. Her teacher said that the lemmings had a chemical in them similar to antifreeze in their blood, that kept them active all winter when other little mammals were hibernating. "They eat grass and multiply all winter," Mrs. Franklin had said in her singsong voice. "When there are too many, they grow nervous at the sight of each other. Somehow this shoots too much antifreeze into their bloodstreams and it begins to poison them. They become restless, then crazy. They run in a frenzy until they die."

Of this phenomenon Miyax's father had simply said, "The hour of the lemming is over for four years."

Unfortunately for Miyax, the hour of the animals that prey on the lemmings was also over. The white fox, the snowy owl, the weasel, the jaeger, and the siskin had virtually disappeared. They had no food to eat and bore few or no young. Those that lived preyed on each other. With the passing of the lemmings, however, the grasses had grown high again and the hour of the caribou was upon the land. Healthy fat caribou cows gave birth to many calves. The caribou population increased, and this in turn increased the number of wolves who prey on the caribou. The abundance of the big deer of the north did Miyax no good, for she had not brought a gun on her trip. It had never occurred to her that she would not reach Point Hope before her food ran out.

A dull pain seized her stomach. She pulled blades of grass from their sheaths and ate the sweet ends. They were not very satisfying, so she picked a handful of caribou moss, a lichen. If the deer could survive in winter on this food, why not she? She munched, decided the plant might taste better if cooked, and went to the pond for water.

As she dipped her pot in, she thought about Amaroq. Why had he bared his teeth at her? Because she was young and he knew she couldn't hurt him? No, she said to herself, it was because he was speaking to her! He had told her to lie down. She had even understood and obeyed him. He had talked to her not with his voice, but with his ears, eyes, and lips; and he had even commended her with a wag of his tail.

She dropped her pot, scrambled up the frost heave, and stretched out on her stomach.

"Amaroq," she called softly, "I understand what you said. Can you understand me? I'm hungry—very, very hungry. Please bring me some meat."

The great wolf did not look her way and she began to doubt her reasoning. After all, flattened ears and a tail-wag were scarcely a conversation. She dropped her forehead against the lichens and rethought what had gone between them.

"Then why did I lie down?" she asked, lifting her head and looking at Amaroq. "Why did I?" she called to the yawning wolves. Not one turned her way.

Amaroq got to his feet, and as he slowly arose he seemed to fill the sky and blot out the sun. He was enormous. He could swallow her without even chewing.

"But he won't," she reminded herself. "Wolves do not eat people. That's gussak talk. Kapugen said wolves are gentle brothers."

The black puppy was looking at her and wagging his tail. Hopefully, Miyax held out a pleading hand to him. His tail wagged harder. The mother rushed to him and stood above him sternly. When he licked her cheek apologetically, she pulled back her lips from her fine white teeth. They flashed as she smiled and forgave her cub.

"But don't let it happen again," said Miyax sarcastically, mimicking her own elders. The mother walked toward Amaroq.

"I should call you Martha after my stepmother," Miyax whispered. "But you're much too beautiful. I shall call you Silver instead."

Silver moved in a halo of light, for the sun sparkled on the guard hairs that grew out over the dense underfur and she seemed to glow.

The reprimanded pup snapped at a crane fly and shook himself. Bits of lichen and grass spun off his fur. He reeled unsteadily, took a wider stance, and looked down at his sleeping sister. With a yap he jumped on her and rolled her to her feet. She whined. He barked and picked up a bone. When he was sure she was watching, he ran down the slope with it. The sister tagged after him. He stopped and she grabbed the bone, too. She pulled; he pulled; then he pulled and she yanked.

Miyax could not help laughing. The puppies played with bones like Eskimo children played with leather ropes.

"I understand *that*," she said to the pups. "That's tug-o-war. Now how do you say, 'I'm hungry'?"

Amaroq was pacing restlessly along the crest of the frost heave as if something were about to happen. His eyes shot to Silver, then to the gray wolf Miyax had named Nails. These glances seemed to be a summons, for Silver and Nails glided to him, spanked the ground with their forepaws, and bit him gently under the chin. He wagged his tail furiously and took Silver's slender nose in his mouth. She crouched before him, licked his cheek, and lovingly bit his lower jaw. Amaroq's tail flashed high as her mouthing charged him with vitality. He nosed her affectionately. Unlike the fox who met his mate only in the breeding season, Amaroq lived with his mate all year.

Next, Nails took Amaroq's jaw in his mouth and the leader bit the top of his nose. A third adult, a small male, came slinking up. He got down on his belly before Amaroq, rolled trembling to his back, and wriggled.

"Hello, Jello," Miyax whispered, for he reminded her of a quivering gussak dessert her mother-in-law made.

She had seen the wolves mouth Amaroq's chin twice before and so she concluded that it was a ceremony, a sort of "Hail to the Chief." He must indeed be their leader for he was so clearly the wealthy wolf; that is, wealthy as she had known the meaning of the word on Nunivak Island. There the old Eskimo hunters she had known in her childhood thought the riches of life were intelligence, fearlessness, and love. A man with these gifts was rich and was a great spirit who was admired in the same way that the gussaks admired a man with money and goods.

The three adults paid tribute to Amaroq until he was almost smothered with love; then he bayed a wild note that sounded like the wind on the frozen sea. With that the others sat around him, the puppies scattered between them. Jello hunched forward and Silver shot a fierce glance at him. Intimidated, Jello pulled his ears together and back. He drew himself down until he looked smaller than ever.

Amaroq wailed again, stretching his neck until his head was high above the others. They gazed at him affectionately and it was plain to see that he was their great spirit, a royal leader who held his group together with love and wisdom.

Any fear Miyax had of the wolves was dispelled by their affection for each other. They were friendly animals and so devoted to Amaroq that she needed only to be accepted by him to be accepted by all. She even knew how to achieve this—bite him under the chin. But how was she going to do that?

She studied the pups hoping they had a simpler way of expressing their love for him. The black puppy approached the leader, sat, then lay down and wagged his tail vigorously. He gazed up at Amaroq in pure adoration, and the royal eyes softened.

Well, that's what I'm doing! Miyax thought. She called to Amaroq. "I'm lying down gazing at you, too, but you don't look at *me* that way!"

When all the puppies were wagging his praises, Amaroq yipped, hit a high note, and crooned. As his voice rose and fell, the other adults sang out and the puppies yipped and bounced.

The song ended abruptly. Amaroq arose and trotted swiftly down the slope. Nails followed, and behind him ran Silver, then Jello. But Jello did not run far. Silver turned and looked him straight in the eye. She pressed her ears forward aggressively and lifted her tail. With that, Jello went back to the puppies and the three sped away like dark birds.

Miyax hunched forward on her elbows, the better to see and learn. She now knew how to be a good puppy, pay tribute to the leader, and even to be a leader by biting others on the top of the nose. She also knew how to tell Jello to baby-sit. If only she had big ears and a tail, she could lecture and talk to them all.

Flapping her hands on her head for ears, she flattened her fingers to make friends, pulled them together and back to express fear, and shot them forward to display her aggression and dominance. Then she folded her arms and studied the puppies again.

The black one greeted Jello by tackling his feet. Another jumped on his tail, and before he could discipline either, all five were upon him. He rolled and tumbled with them for almost an hour; then he ran down the slope, turned, and stopped. The pursuing pups plowed into him, tumbled, fell, and lay still. During a minute of surprised recovery there was no action. Then the black pup flashed his tail like a semaphore signal and they all jumped on Jello again.

Miyax rolled over and laughed aloud. "That's funny. They're really like kids."

When she looked back, Jello's tongue was hanging from his mouth and his sides were heaving. Four of the puppies had collapsed at his feet and were asleep. Jello flopped down, too, but the black pup still looked around. He was not the least bit tired. Miyax watched him, for there was something special about him.

He ran to the top of the den and barked. The smallest pup, whom Miyax called Sister, lifted her head, saw her favorite brother in action and, struggling to her feet, followed him devotedly. While they romped, Jello took the opportunity to rest behind a clump of sedge, a moisture-loving plant of the tundra. But hardly was he settled before a pup tracked him to his hideout and pounced on him. Jello narrowed his eyes, pressed his ears forward, and showed his teeth.

"I know what you're saying," she called to him. "You're saying, 'lie down.'" The puppy lay down, and Miyax got on all fours and looked for the nearest pup to speak to. It was Sister.

"Ummmm," she whined, and when Sister turned around Julie narrowed her eyes and showed her white teeth. Obediently, Sister lay down.

"I'm talking wolf! I'm talking wolf!" Miyax clapped, and tossing her head like a pup, crawled in a happy circle. As she was coming back she saw all five puppies sitting in a row watching her, their heads cocked in curiosity. Boldly the black pup came toward her, his fat backside swinging as he trotted to the bottom of her frost heave, and barked.

"You are *very* fearless and *very* smart," she said. "Now I know why you are special. You are wealthy and the leader of the puppies. There is no doubt what you'll grow up to be. So I shall name you after my father Kapugen, and I shall call you Kapu for short."

Kapu wrinkled his brow and turned an ear to tune in more acutely on her voice.

"You don't understand, do you?"

Hardly had she spoken than his tail went up, his mouth opened slightly, and he fairly grinned.

"Ee-lie!" she gasped. "You do understand. And that scares me." She perched on her heels. Jello whined an undulating note and Kapu turned back to the den.

Miyax imitated the call to come home. Kapu looked back over his shoulder in surprise. She giggled. He wagged his tail and jumped on Jello.

She clapped her hands and settled down to watch this language of jumps and tumbles, elated that she was at last breaking the wolf code. After a long time she decided that they were not talking but roughhousing, and so she started home. Later she changed her mind. Roughhousing was very important to wolves. It occupied almost the entire night for the pups.

"Ee-lie, okay," she said. "I'll learn to roughhouse. Maybe then you'll accept me and feed me." She pranced, jumped, and whimpered; she growled, snarled, and rolled. But nobody came to roughhouse.

Sliding back to her camp, she heard the grass swish and looked up to see Amaroq and his hunters sweep around her frost heave and stop about five feet away. She could smell the sweet scent of their fur.

The hairs on her neck rose and her eyes widened. Amaroq's ears went forward aggressively and she remembered that wide eyes meant fear to him. It was not good to show him she was afraid. Animals attacked the fearful. She tried to narrow them, but remembered that was not right either. Narrowed eyes were mean. In desperation she recalled that Kapu had moved forward when challenged. She pranced right up to Amaroq. Her heart beat furiously as she grunt-whined the sound of the puppy begging adoringly for attention. Then she got down on her belly and gazed at him with fondness.

The great wolf backed up and avoided her eyes. She had said something wrong! Perhaps even offended him. Some slight gesture that meant nothing to her apparently meant something to the wolf. His ears shot forward angrily and it seemed all was lost. She wanted to get up and run, but she gathered her courage and pranced closer to him. Swiftly she patted him under the chin.

The signal went off. It sped through his body and triggered emotions of love. Amaroq's ears flattened and his tail wagged in friendship. He could not react in any other way to the chin pat, for the roots of this signal lay deep in wolf history. It was inherited from generations and generations of leaders before him. As his eyes softened, the sweet odor of ambrosia arose from the gland on the top of his tail and she was drenched lightly in wolf scent. Miyax was one of the pack.

ALL THROUGH THE SUNNY NIGHT she waited for Amaroq to come home with food for her and the pups. When at last she saw him on the horizon she got down on all fours and crawled to her lookout. He carried no food.

"Ayi," she cried. "The pups must be nursing—that's why there's no meat." Slumping back on her heels, she thought about this. Then she thought again.

"You can't be nursing," she said to Kapu, and plunked her hands on her hips. "Silver growls when you suckle, and drives you away." Kapu twisted his ears at the sound of her voice.

"Okay," she called to him. "Where are you getting the food that makes you so fat?" He ignored her, concentrating on Silver and Nails, who were coming home from the hunt.

Miyax went back to her pot and stuffed on the cold raw moss until her stomach felt full if not satisfied. Then she crawled into her cozy home in the hope that sleep would soothe her hunger.

She smoothed the silver hairs of her beautiful wedding parka, then carefully took it off and rolled it up. Placing it and her fur pants in a bag made of whale bladder, she tied it securely so that no moisture would dampen her clothes while she slept. This she had learned in childhood, and it was one of the old Eskimo ways that she liked, perhaps the only one. She had never violated it, even in the warm, gas-heated house in Barrow, for damp clothes could mean death in the Arctic.

When her outer garments were put away she took off the bright-red tights her mother-in-law had bought for her at the American store in Barrow. Walking to the pond, she rinsed them and laid them in the sun. The cool air struck her naked body. She shivered and was glad that she had done one thing right—she had worn her winter clothes, not her light summer *kuspuck*, the woman's dress.

The wind gusted; Miyax scrambled through the low door and slid into her sleeping skin. The silken softness of the rabbit fur embraced her and she pulled the hood around her face so that only her nose was exposed. The fur captured her warm breath, held it against her face, and she became her own radiant stove. In this cozy micro-world she forgot her hunger and recalled what she already knew about wolves so that she could put it together with what she had observed.

Wolves are shy, Kapugen had said, and they desert their dens if discovered by man; yet this pack had not. Did Amaroq not know she was human? Perhaps not; she had never walked in his presence, the two-legged signal of "man" to wild animals. On the other hand, he must know. Kapugen had said that with one sniff a wolf knew if you were male or female, adult or child, if you were hunting or not hunting—even if you were happy or sad. She concluded that Amaroq tolerated her because she was young, had no gun, and was sad—a lost child.

She next considered Nails. Who was he? Amaroq's dependable friend, that was true, yet she suspected he was even more than that—a spiritual father of the pups. Nails took orders from Amaroq, but stayed close to Silver and the little wolves. He was father when their real father was busy. He was Amaroq's serious partner. But Jello? Who was he? Where had he come from? Was he a pup of a previous year? Or had he joined the pack just as she had, by soliciting Amaroq for membership in his tribe? There was much to learn about her family.

Miyax did not know how long she slept, for midnight was almost as bright as noon and it was difficult to judge the passing of time. It did not matter, however; time in the Arctic was the rhythm of life. The wolf pups were barking their excited *yipoo* that rang out the hour of the end of the hunt. The pack was coming home. With visions of caribou stew in her head, she got out of her sleeping skin and reached for her clothes.

The puppies may not have been eating, but certainly Amaroq would have to bring Jello some food. He had been home all night. Stepping into the sunlight, she put on her tights, danced a moment, and then pulled on her furs. Leaning over the pond, she saw in the glassy water the hollows of her cheeks. She was pleased, for she looked almost like the gussak girls in the magazines and movies—thin and gaunt, not moon-faced like an Eskimo. Her hair! She leaned closer to the tundra looking glass. Her hair was a mess. Pressing it into place with her hands, she wished she had taken Daniel's wedding brush and comb with her. They lay unused in the corner of a table drawer in the house at Barrow.

Quickly she climbed the frost heave, lay down, and looked at the wolves. There was no meat to be seen. The three hunters were stretched out on their sides, their bellies extended with food. Jello was gone. Of course, she said to herself, he had been relieved of his duties and had backtracked the hunters to the kill. She winced, for she had been so certain that today she would eat. So I won't, she said to herself, and that's that.

Miyax knew when to stop dreaming and be practical. She slid down the heave, brushed off her parka, and faced the tundra. The plants around the pond had edible seeds, as did the many grasses. There were thousands of crane fly and mosquito larvae in the water, and the wild-flowers were filling if not very nourishing. But they were all small and took time to gather. She looked around for something bigger.

Her black eyes were alert as several Lapland longspurs darted over-head. They might still have young in their nests. Staying on one side of the heave, so the wolves would not see her two-leggedness, she skipped into the grass. The birds vanished. Their dark pointed wings were erased from the sky as if they had sensed her deadly purpose. Miyax crouched down. Kapugen had taught her how to hunt birds by sitting still and being patient. She crossed her feet and blended into the plants, still as a stone.

Presently a grass blade trembled and Miyax saw a young bird flut-tering its wings as it begged to be fed. A brown lark-like parent winged down and stuffed its open beak. Another youngster begged and the parent flew to it. Unfortunately, the second little bird was so far from the first that Miyax knew they were out of the nest and im-possible to catch. She shifted her attention to the snow buntings.

A movement in the sky above the horizon caught her attention, and she recognized the pointed tail and black head of a jaeger. She knew this bird well, for it hunted the shore and tundra of Nunivak Island. A bold sea bird, it resembled its close relative the gull, but was not a fisher. The jaeger preyed upon lemmings, small birds, and occasionally carrion. Miyax wondered what prey it was hunting. Three more jaegers joined the first, circled close together as if over a target, then dropped out of sight below the horizon.

"The wolf kill!" she fairly shouted. "They're sharing the wolf kill."

Jumping to her feet, she lined up the spot where they had disappeared with a patch of brown lichens in the distance, and ran with joy along the invisible line. When she had gone a quarter of a mile, she stopped and looked back. The endless tundra rolled around her and she could not tell which frost heave was which.

"Oh, no!" she cried. She turned around and laboriously searched out the plants crushed by her feet. Near a pool she lost all sight of her steps and then with relief recognized an empty lemming nest, a round ball of grass that she had kicked open. She pounced on it, saw a flower she had trampled, and ran up the heave to it. From the top she looked across the distance to her own precious house.

She reminded herself not to be so careless again. "One can get lost out here," she said aloud.

Miyax flopped down on the grass to rest. Her hand touched a patch of Arctic peas. They were tiny but numerous; she took off her boot and then her sock, and filled its toe with the vegetables. When all were harvested, she swung the sock over her shoulder and, striding joyously, rounded her pond and plunked the peas in her pot. She rolled them around with her fingers and they rattled musically. She rolled them again and made up words to fit their rhythm:

> *Peas that go* tink, *peas that go* tot,
> *Peas that will never grow outside my pot.*

The puppies yapped and Silver ran out across the tundra. She leaped with grace, her fur gleaming like metal; then she swept into a dip in the landscape and vanished. Up from the horizon rose the jaegers, announcing that Silver had gone to the kill. Clutching the cooking pot to her breast, Miyax excitedly waited to see her bring back meat for the pups.

The jaegers circled, the longspurs tumbled on their wings, and at last Silver came home. Her mouth was empty.

"I just don't understand," she said to the pups. "What is keeping you alive?" Putting down her pot, she went to her lookout to try to solve the riddle.

Silver came up the long slope, gave the grunt-whine that summoned the pups, and Kapu ran to meet her. She pulled back her lips in a smile and nosed him affectionately. Then Kapu stuck his nose in the corner of her mouth. Silver arched her back, her neck rippled, and she choked up a big mound of meat. Kapu set upon it with a snarl.

"So that's it!" said Miyax. "The meat's in the belly-basket. Now what do I do?"

Kapu let Sister share the meal with him, but not Zing, Zat, and Zit—as Miyax had dubbed the three tawny pups who had little personality as yet. Zing rushed over to the resting Silver and cuddled up against her. He rammed his nose against her teats and taking one in his mouth, ravenously nursed. Silver tolerated this for a moment, then growled. He did not let go and she snapped at him. He pulled away, but when she stretched out he dove back into her belly fur again. With a loud bark she rolled onto her stomach and cut off her milk from him. Zing got up, walked over to Amaroq, and stuck his nose in the corner of his mouth. Amaroq regurgitated food.

The secret of the fat pups was out. They were being weaned from mother's milk to well-chewed and partially digested food.

They might eat food from the belly-basket for weeks before they were brought chunks of meat that Miyax could share, and so she went out into the grasses again to look for buntings. Soon Silver and Nails trotted off in the direction of the kill. Having fed the puppies, they were now feeding themselves. Miyax cautiously peered around the heave. Jello had not gone with them. Yet he had been to the kill. He would have food in his belly-basket.

When the jaegers arose into the air she picked up the pot and climbed once again to the top of her frost heave. Getting to her hands and knees, she gave a grunt-whine call. "Look at me, I'm nice," it said.

Jello strode toward her. So pushed around was he by Silver, so respectful of Amaroq and even Nails, that he was excited by a voice more humble than his own. He even lifted his tail and head higher than Miyax had ever seen him do, and, acting like the boss wolf, loped up her frost heave. Curious Kapu trotted behind.

As Miyax scurried to meet Jello, he hesitated, growled softly, and urinated. "Don't be scared," she said and whimpered. He circled closer. Quickly rising to her knees, grunting the note of friendship, she slipped her hand over his head and clasped the top of his nose firmly in her fingers.

"I'm boss," she said as his tail and head went down in deference to the symbol of leadership. She started to slip her hand into the corner of his mouth, but he jerked away. Then Kapu, as if he understood what Miyax wanted, swept up to Jello and nuzzled his mouth. Jello heaved, opened his jaws, and deposited food on the ground.

"I'll live! I'll live!" Miyax cried jubilantly as Jello turned, put his tail between his legs, and raced back to the other pups. Kapu sat down and watched with wrinkled forehead as she scooped the meat into the pot. When she had retrieved every morsel, she gently closed her lips on the bridge of his nose. His tail wagged respectfully and he gazed softly into her eyes.

"Kapu," she whispered. "We Eskimos have joking partners—people to have fun with—and serious partners—people to work and think with. You and I are both. We are joking-serious partners." He wagged his tail excitedly and blinked. "And that's the best of all." She reached out to hug him, for his eyes were mellow and his fuzz irresistible. But he was like water and slipped through her hands.

On two knees and one hand, holding the pot with the other, Miyax hobbled toward her camp. Kapu bit her heel softly and she glanced over her shoulder. His head was cocked and his tail swished slowly.

"What are you saying now?" she asked. He gave the grunt-whine for attention.

Of course, she was his big sister and he wanted to play. Reaching into her pocket she pulled out a mitten and before she could flash it in front of his nose, he had leaped, caught it, and was pulling and shaking her whole arm and torso with incredible strength.

Miyax let go lest she spill her meat, and Kapu rolled head over heels into the lichens. Taking a firm grip on the mitten, he flattened his ears in spirited fellowship, dashed down the slope and up to his den. There he turned to see if she was following.

"Bring back my mitten," she called. "I need it." He flashed his wolf smile of apology, shook the mitten, and romped into the midst of his other brothers.

Kapu scratched a wide swath on the ground with his hind feet. The three tawny pups sniffed the mark and Zit sat down before it. Bold Kapu had written his signature and it was deep and impressive. Miyax wondered if the mitten victory was responsible. It was quite a trophy to win.

Placing her pot by the fireplace, she walked out on the tundra and gathered dry grass and lichens in her sock, for there was, of course, no wood to burn. Although caribou droppings were a better fuel, she was too fearful of getting lost to hunt them. Piling the grass and lichens in the center of the stones, she went into her house, took a small cookie tin from her pack, and removed one precious match. Then she lit the tinder.

The grass burst into flame and the lichens smoldered slowly, giving her time to dig the peat that the dead grasses had laid down for thousands and thousands of years. Gradually the peat glowed, the water boiled, and an hour later Miyax had a pot of caribou stew.

"At last!" she said. On it floated great chunks of golden grease, more delicious than the butter from the gussak store. She put a savory bite in her mouth, sucked the juices, then chewed a long time before she swallowed. She must not eat too fast or too much. Kapugen had said that an old lady, rescued from the snow after weeks of starvation, so stuffed herself that she died the next day.

Munching another bite, she went out to the grass clump to check on buntings, and a long time later returned to eat two more chunks of caribou. The rest, though she longed for it, she stored inside her house. Then she patted her stomach and told it to wait.

For the first time in days she could think of something other than food. Her mind turned to the problem of which direction was north and in which direction lay the town of Point Hope. The dips and heaves of the tundra spread out all around her and still looked the same in every direction.

"Oh, ho!" she said aloud. "More lichens grow on one side of the frost heaves than on the other." She pondered this, as well as the oblong shape of her pond, which was caused by the flow of the ice as it moved with the wind. But did the wind come down from the north or out of the west on the North Slope of Alaska? She did not know. Next, she noted that the grasses grew in different spots than the mosses, and the more she studied, the more the face of the tundra emerged; a face that could tell her which way was north, if she had listened more carefully to Kapugen.

Her legs began to buckle and her body swayed. She crumpled to her knees, for the food was making her both dizzy and sleepy. She staggered into her fur-carpeted house and lay down.

Mıyax's eyelids fluttered; the black lashes parted, then framed her wide eyes like ferns around a pool. She had eaten, slept for many hours; and the dull, tired feeling of starvation was gone. She felt bright and very much alive.

Rolling to her stomach, she propped herself on her elbows, and reached into her pot to eat. She ate a lot. The food in the pot lowered drastically. When but two meals remained, she made up her mind to tell Amaroq she wanted a whole shank of caribou. Wolves did bring food to their dens. Kapugen had seen them walk long miles in spring, with legs and ribs for the mothers who stayed in the ground with their pups for almost ten days after birth.

Well, she had no puppies to induce Amaroq to feed her, so she pondered again. Kapugen had once told her of a wolf who was wounded by the hoofs of a caribou. He limped to a rock cave and lay down to recover. Every night his leader trotted over the snow, bringing him meat until he was well and could rejoin the pack.

Miyax did not want to suffer a wound, but it seemed to her that in order to be fed by wolves one had to be helpless.

"If that's the case," she said to herself, "I should be buried in food. I'm helpless enough. I cannot fell a caribou or catch a bird. And I'm lost, besides." She thrust her head out the door.

"Amaroq, I'm helpless," she cried. The chilly air tingled her nose and she noticed that the cotton grasses by the pond were seeding out into white puffs. This was worrisome, for they marked the coming of autumn, the snows, and the white-outs. White-outs could be dangerous. When the cotton grass heads were gone, the winds would lift the snow from the ground to the air and she would not be able to see her feet. She would be imprisoned wherever she stood . . . maybe for days . . . maybe till death.

Amaroq howled the long note to assemble. Silver and Nails barked a brief "Coming," and it was the beginning of a new day for Miyax and the wolves. Although the clocks in Barrow would say it was time to get ready for bed, she was getting up, for she was on wolf time. Since there was no darkness to hamper her vision, night was as good a time to work as day, and much better if you were a wolf girl. Rehearsing whimpers and groveling positions as she climbed to her lookout, she got ready to tell Amaroq how helpless she was in his own language.

He was awake, lying on his side, watching Sister's paw twitch as she slept. He got up and licked the restless sleeper as if to say "All's well." The paw relaxed.

Miyax whimpered and twisted her head appealingly. Amaroq shot her a glance and wagged his tail as if she had said "Hello," not "I'm helpless."

Suddenly his head lifted, his ears went up, and Amaroq sniffed the wind. Miyax sniffed the wind and smelled nothing, although Amaroq was on his feet now, electric with the airborne message. He snapped his hunters to attention and led them down the slope and off across the tundra. Jello stayed home with the pups.

The pack moved in single file almost to the horizon, then swerved and came back. Shading her eyes, Miyax finally saw what the wind had told Amaroq. A heard of caribou was passing through. She held her breath as the hunters sped toward a large buck. The animal opened his stride and gracefully gained ground. He could so easily outrun the wolves that Amaroq let him go and trotted toward another. This one, too, outdistanced the pack and Amaroq swerved and tested another. Just as Miyax was wondering how the wolves ever caught anything, Amaroq put on full speed and bore down on a third.

This animal could not outrun him, and when Amaroq attacked he turned and struck with his powerful hoofs. Like a bouncing ball the leader sprang away. Nails and Silver fanned out to either side of the beast, then veered and closed in. The caribou bellowed, pressed back his ears, zigzagged over a frost heave, and disappeared from sight.

"They're chasing the weakest," Miyax said in astonishment. "It's just like Kapugen said—wolves take the old and sick."

She looked from the empty tundra to the busy den sight. Kapu was staring at her, his eyes narrowed, his ears thrown forward aggressively.

"Now why are you so hostile?" she asked, then looked at her feet and legs. "Ee-lie, Ee-lie." She dropped to all fours and smiled apologetically.

"Ayi, Kapu. You've never seen a man in all your life. What is it that tells you to beware? Some spirit of your ancestors that still dwells in your body?"

She gave the grunt-whine and Kapu pressed down his ears, snatched up a bone, and brought it over to her. She grabbed it, he tugged, she pulled, he growled, she giggled, and Jello called Kapu home. He cocked an ear, rolled his eyes, and ignored the baby-sitter.

"You're naughty," she said and covered a grin with her hand. "Martha would scold me for that."

Kapu dropped the bone. She leaned down, picked it up in her teeth, and tried to run on all fours. She had barely begun to move away when Kapu leaped on her back and took her bare neck in his teeth. She started to scream, checked herself and, closing her eyes, waited for the teeth to pierce her skin. They did not even bruise, so controlled was this grip that said "Drop the bone." She let it go, and in one swish Kapu leaped to the ground and snatched it.

As she started after him something struck her boot and she looked around to see Zit, Zat, and Sister at her heels. Zing charged up the knoll, hit her arm with great force, and knocked her to the ground. She growled, flashed her teeth, and narrowed her eyes. Kapu dropped the bone and lay down. Zing backed up, and for a moment not a puppy moved.

"Phew." She smiled. "That did it."

Too late she remembered that such a smile was an apology, a sort of "I didn't mean it," and before she could growl all five little wolves jumped on her again.

"Stop!" She was angry. They sensed it and backed away. "Shoo! Go!" She waved her arm above her head and the threatening pose spoke louder than all her words. Dropping their tails, glancing warily at her, they trotted away—all but Kapu. He licked her cheek.

"Dear Kapu." She was about to stroke his head, when he picked up the bone and carried it back to the den. But he was not done with play. He never was. Kapu was tireless. Diving into a tunnel, he came out on the other side and landed on Jello's tail.

When Miyax saw this she sat back on her heels. Open-ended tunnels reminded her of something. In the spring, wolf packs stay at a nursery den where the pups are born deep in the earth at the end of long tunnels. When the pups are about six weeks old and big enough to walk and run, the leaders move the entire group to a summer den. These are mere shelters for the pups and are open at two ends. For a few weeks the packs stay at this den; then they leave and take up the nomadic winter life of the wolf.

The cold chill of fear ran up Miyax's spine—the wolves would soon depart! Then what would she do? She could not follow them; they often ran fifty miles in a night and slept in different spots each day.

Her hands trembled and she pressed them together to make them stop, for Kapugen had taught her that fear can so cripple a person that he cannot think or act. Already she was too scared to crawl.

"Change your ways when fear seizes," he had said, "for it usually means you are doing something wrong."

She knew what it was—she should not depend upon the wolves for survival. She must go on her own. Instantly she felt relieved, her legs moved, her hands stopped shaking, and she remembered that when Kapugen was a boy, he had told her, he made snares of rawhide and caught little birds.

"Buntings beware!" she shouted and slid down to her camp. Stepping out of her pants, she slipped off her tights and cut a swath of cloth from the hip with her ulo. She tore the cloth into small strips, then ate some stew, and started off to hunt birds. Every so often she tied a bit of red cloth to a clump of grass or around a conspicuous stone. If she was going to hunt in this confusing land, she must leave a trail to lead her home. She could not smell her way back as the wolves did.

As she tied the first piece of cloth to a bent sedge, she looked down at a small pile of droppings. "Ee-lie," she said. "A bird roost. Someone sleeps here every night." Quickly she took the thongs from her boots, made a noose, and placed it under the sedge. Holding the pull-rope, she moved back as far as she could and lay down to await the return of the bird.

The sun slid slowly down the sky, hung still for a moment, then started up again. It was midnight. A flock of swift-flying Arctic terns darted overhead, and one by one dropped into the grasses. Ruddy turnstones called sleepily from their scattered roosts, and sandpipers whistled. The creatures of the tundra were going to sleep, as they did also at noon in the constant daylight. Each called from his roost—all but the little bird of the sedge. It had not come back.

A bird chirped three feet from her face, and Miyax rolled her eyes to the left. A bunting on a grass blade tucked its bill into the feathers on its back, fluffed, and went to sleep. Where, she asked, was the bird of the sedge? Had it been killed by a fox or a weasel?

She was about to get to her feet and hunt elsewhere, but she remembered that Kapugen never gave up. Sometimes he would stand motionless for five hours at a seal breathing hole in the ice waiting for a seal to come up for a breath. She must wait, too.

The sun moved on around the sky and, when it was directly behind her, the sleeping bunting lifted its head and chirped. It hopped to a higher blade of grass, preened, and sang its morning song. The sleep was over. Her bird had not come back.

Suddenly a shadow passed. A snowy owl, white wings folded in a plummeting dive, threw out his feathered feet and struck the little gray bunting. The owl bounced up, and came down almost on Miyax's outstretched hand, the bird caught in his foot. Her first instinct was to pounce on the owl, but she instantly thought better of that. Even if she could catch him, she would have his powerful claws and beak to contend with, and she knew what damage they could do. Besides, she had a better idea—to lie still and watch where he flew. Perhaps he had owlets in the nest, for these little birds took almost six weeks to get on their wings. If there were owlets, there would also be food, lots of it, for the male owls are constantly bringing food to the young. Once, she had counted eight lemmings piled at the nest of a snowy owl.

So close was the *ukpik*, the white owl of the north, that she could see the clove markings on his wings and the dense white feathers that covered his legs and feet. His large yellow eyes were pixieish, and he looked like a funny little Eskimo in white parka and maklaks. The wind stirred the wolverine trim on Miyax's hood and the owl turned his gleaming eyes upon her. She tried not to blink and belie the life in her stone-still body, but he was suspicious. He turned his head almost upside down to get a more acute focus on her; then unwinding swiftly, he lifted his body and sped off. His wings arched deeply as he steered into a wind and shot like a bullet toward the sun. As Miyax rolled to a sitting position, the owl scooped his wings up, braked, and dropped onto an exceptionally large frost heave. He left the bird and flew out over the tundra, screaming the demonic call of the hunting ukpik.

Miyax tied another red patch on the sedge, rounded a boggy pond, and climbed the heave where the owl lived. There lay an almost dead owlet, its big beak resting on the edge of the stone-lined nest. It lifted its head, laboriously hissed, and collapsed. The owlet was starving, for there was only the bunting, when there should have been dozens of lemmings. It would not live, in this time of no lemmings.

She picked up the bunting and owlet, regretting that she had found a provider only to lose him again. The male owl would not bring food to an empty nest.

Collecting her red markers as she walked home, she kicked open old lemming nests in the hope of finding baby weasels. These small relatives of the mink, with their valuable fur that turns white in winter, enter lemming nests and kill and eat the young. Then they move into the round grassy structures to give birth to their own young. Although Miyax kicked seven nests, there were no weasels—for there were no lemmings to eat.

When in sight of her house she took a shortcut and came upon a pile of old caribou droppings—fuel for her fire! Gleefully, she stuffed her pockets, tied a marker at the site for later use, and skipped home dreaming of owlet stew.

She plucked the birds, laid them on the ground, and skillfully cut them open with her ulo. Lifting out the warm viscera, she tipped back her head and popped them into her mouth. They were delicious— the nuts and candy of the Arctic. She had forgotten how good they tasted. They were rich in vitamins and minerals and her starving body welcomed them.

Treats over, she sliced her birds into delicate strips and simmered them slowly and not too long.

"Chicken of the North," Miyax gave a toast to the birds. Then she drank the rich juices and popped the tender meat in her mouth. Had she been a boy this day would be one to celebrate. When a boy caught his first bird in Nunivak, he was supposed to fast for a day, then celebrate the Feast of the Bird. When he killed his first seal his mother took off her rings, for he was a man, and this was her way of bragging without saying a word.

Silly, she said to herself, but nevertheless she sang Kapugen's song of the Bird Feast.

Tornait, tornait,
*Spirit of the bird,*
*Fly into my body*
*And bring me*
*The power of the sun.*

Kapu yapped to say that the hunters were coming home, and Miyax washed out her pot and went to her lookout to tell them goodnight. Amaroq and Jello were facing each other, ruffs up, ready to fight. Before Jello could attack, Amaroq lifted his head and Jello bowed before him. The dispute was over. No blood was shed. The difference had been settled with the pose of leadership.

Miyax wondered what had happened to put them at odds with each other. Whatever the problem, Jello had surrendered. He was on his back flashing the white fur on his belly that signaled "I give up!"—and no one, not even the pups, could strike him.

"The white flag of surrender," she murmured. "Jello lost." Amaroq walked gracefully away.

He was not done with what he had to say, however. With a dash, he picked up her mitten and tore it to shreds, then rolled in its many pieces and stood up. Nails, Silver, and the pups sniffed him and wagged their tails in great excitement. Then Amaroq narrowed his eyes and glanced her way. With a chill she realized he was going to attack. She flattened herself like an obedient pup as he glided down his slope and up hers. Her breathing quickened, her heart raced.

When Amaroq was but five feet away and she could see each hair on his long fine nose, he gave the grunt-whine. He was calling her! Cautiously she crawled toward him. He wagged his tail and led her down the hill, through the sedges, and up the long slope to the wolf den. Patiently adjusting his stride to her clumsy crawl he brought her home to the pack, perhaps against Jello's will—she would never know.

At the den site he promptly ignored her and went to his bed, a dish-like scoop in the soil on the highest point. Circling three or four times, scratching the earth to prepare it for sleep, he lay down.

Miyax glanced out of the corner of her eyes to see Nails preparing his bed also with scratches and turns. Silver was already in her scoop, snapping at the nursing Zing. Jello was off by himself.

Now it was Miyax's turn to say she was home. Patting the ground, circling first to the left and then to the right, she lay down and pulled her knees up to her chin. She closed her eyes, but not completely.

Through her lashes she peeked at Amaroq for reassurance, just as she had seen the other wolves do. The wind played across his black ruff and his ears twitched from time to time as he listened to the birds and winds in his sleep. All was well with the world, and apparently with her, for Amaroq rested in peace.

But Miyax could not sleep. The sun reached its apogee and started down the blue sky of early afternoon. The elegant Arctic terns cut swirls in the sky, a spider crept under a stone, and the snow buntings flitted and called. From some distant spot a loon cried. Then the pale green of evening was upon the land and Miyax closed her eyes.

She awoke with a start a short time later and looked about in puzzlement. The sky vaulted above her. A grass blade tickled her face, and she remembered where she was—up on the frost heave with the wolf pack! Breathing deeply to quell a sense of uneasiness, she finally relaxed, unrolled, and sat up. Kapu was curled against her leg. His feet were flipping and he yipped as if challenging some wolf badman in his dreams. Softly she stroked his fur.

"All's well," she whispered and his paws stopped moving. He sighed and dreamed on peacefully.

She glanced around. All of the wolves were asleep, although they usually went hunting when the sky was lime-green. Perhaps they knew something she didn't know. Sniffing and turning her head, she saw nothing different from any other evening. Then in the distance a thick wall of fog arose. It blotted out the horizon, the far dips and heaves, the grasses, the pond, and finally her own frost heave. The fog streamed up the wolf slope and enveloped the members of the pack one by one until only Kapu was visible. Fogs were part of the Arctic summer, rolling in from the sea for only an hour or for many days, but Miyax had never given them much thought. Now she remembered that when the fog rolled over Barrow, airplanes were grounded, ships and boats had to be anchored, and even the two jeeps in town sat where they had stopped in the fog. She also remembered that people were prisoners of the fog, too. They could not see to hunt.

Now, if the wolves did not bring her some meat, she might not eat for days. She could resort to the belly-basket again, but Jello was jumpy and she doubted if she had enough courage to put her hands in the mouths of the others. Perhaps Kapu would share his meals with her.

"Kapu?" He sighed and pushed tighter against her. The whiskers that protected his sensitive nose and warned him of objects nearby, twitched as her breath touched them. His lips curled up. Whatever he was dreaming about now must be funny, she thought. She hoped so, for her wide-awake dream was hardly amusing—it was desperate.

She was looking at Silver stretched not far away in a thin spot of fog. Zing, the incorrigible Zing, was nursing again. Silver growled. The pup rolled to his back, paws outstretched like an upside-down chair. Then Sister moved out of the fog. She snuggled up to her mother, suckled two or three times, more for comfort than for food, and fell back to sleep.

This brief sucking of the pups had started Silver's milk flowing. Miyax stared at this unexpected source of food.

She inched forward on her stomach and elbows until she was

close to the mother. Miyax had drunk the milk of other wild mammals on Nunivak and each time had found it sweet and good. True, the walrus and musk oxen had been milked by her father, but if he had done it, why couldn't she? Slipping her hand beneath a nipple she caught several drops, keeping her eyes on Silver to discern her mood. Slowly Miyax brought the milk to her mouth, lapped, and found it as rich as butter. She reached out again, but as she did so, Silver closed her jaws on Miyax's shoulder and left her immobile. She stifled a scream.

Suddenly Amaroq appeared and lifted his head. Silver let go. Miyax rubbed her shoulder and crept back to Kapu. He was awake, peering up at her, his head on his paws. When their eyes met, he flipped one ear humorously and Miyax sensed he had been through this too.

"Guess I'm weaned," she said. He wagged his tail.

The fog thickened and, like an eraser on a blackboard, wiped out Amaroq and Silver and the tip of Kapu's tail. She cuddled closer to Kapu, wondering if Amaroq would hunt tonight. After a long time she decided he would not—his family was content and well fed. Not she, however; two drops of milk were scarcely life-sustaining. She patted Kapu, crawled off in the fog, and stood up when she thought she was safely out of sight. Amaroq snarled. She dropped to her knees. His tail beat the ground and she gasped.

"I know you can't see me," she called "so how do you know what I'm doing? Can you hear me stand up?" His tail beat again and she scrambled to her house, awed by the sensitivity of Amaroq. He knew about fogs and the sneaky ways of human beings.

The sedges around her pond were visible if she crawled, and so on hands and knees she rounded the bank, picking seeds, digging up the nut-like roots of the sedges, and snatching crane fly larvae from the water. As she crept she ate. After what seemed like hours of constant foraging she was still hungry—but not starving.

She came back to her house in a fog so thick she could almost hold it in her hands. For long hours she was suspended between sleep and wakefulness. She listened to the birds call to keep in touch with each other in the fog. Like herself they could not smell their food; they needed to see. As time dragged on, she sang to pass the hours. At first she invented rhymes about the tundra and sang them to tunes she had learned at school. When she tired of these melodies she improvised on the songs of her childhood. They were better suited to improvisation, for they had been invented for just this purpose—to pass the hours in creative fun when the weather closed in.

She sang about the wolves, her house, and the little feather flower on her table; and when she had no more to say, she crawled to her door and looked out. The fog was somewhat lighter. She could see the empty pot by her fireplace and, low overhead, a few birds in the sky.

Then an airplane droned in the distance, grew louder, then fainter, then louder again. The pilot was circling, waiting to see if the weather might suddenly clear so he could land. The same thing had happened to her when she was flown from Nunivak to Barrow. As their plane came over the town, a dense fog rolled in and the pilot had circled for almost an hour.

"If we cannot land on this turn," he had finally announced over the intercom, "we will head straight back to Fairbanks." But suddenly the fog had cleared, and they had landed in Barrow.

The sound of the plane grew louder. Through the thinning fog she saw the commercial plane that flew from Fairbanks to Barrow and back. Her heart pounded. If the pilot could see her he might send help. She ran out to wave, but the fog had swirled in again and she could barely see her hand. The engines accelerated, and the plane sped off in what must be the direction of Fairbanks. She listened to its sound and, bending down, drew a line in the soil in the direction it had gone.

"That way should be Fairbanks," she said. "At least I know that much."

Picking up pebbles, she pounded them into the line to make it more permanent, and stood up. "That way," she said, pointing in the opposite direction, "is the coast and Point Hope."

Amaroq howled. Nails barked. Then Amaroq slid into a musical crescendo that Silver joined in. Their voices undulated as each harmonized with the other. Jello's windy voice barked out and, like the beat of drums, the five pups whooped and yipped. Miyax rubbed her chin; something was different about this hunt song. It was eerie and restless. It spoke of things she did not understand and she was frightened.

The fog cleared again and she saw Amaroq, his hunters, and the pups running across the tundra. Even Jello was with them. Were they leaving her? Was this their day to take up the wandering life of the wolves? Was she now on her own? Picking up her red markers, she crawled around her frost heave and frantically gathered the leafy plants that the caribou eat. She stuffed mushroom-like fungi in her pockets, and bits of reindeer moss. She could no longer afford to pass up anything that might be edible.

As she worked on her hands and knees, she felt a rhythmical beat, like the rumble of Eskimo drums. Pressing her ear to the ground she heard the vibration of many feet—a herd of caribou was not far away.

The fog thinned more and Kapu came into view. As alert as an eagle, he was sniffing the wind and wagging his tail as if reading some amusing wolf story. She sniffed too, but for her the pages were blank.

The vibrations in the earth grew stronger; Miyax drew back, as out of the fog came a huge caribou, running her way. His head was out straight and his eyes rolled wildly. At his neck, leaping with the power of an ocean wave, was Amaroq. Nails was diving in and out under his legs, and at his flank dashed Silver. Miyax held her breath, wondering whether to run or dodge.

Then Amaroq jumped, floated in the air for an instant, and sank his teeth into the shoulder of the beast. He hung on while Silver attacked from the side. Then he dropped to the ground as the bull bellowed. The fog closed in briefly, and when it thinned the caribou was poised above Amaroq, his cleaver-like hoofs aimed at his head. There was a low grunt, a flash of hoofs, and the huge feet cut uselessly into the sod; for Amaroq had vaulted into the air again and had sunk his teeth in the animal's back. Snarling, using the weight of his body as a tool, he rode the circling and stumbling beast. Silver leaped in front of the bull trying to trip him or slow him down. Nails had a grip on one hind leg. The caribou bucked, writhed, then dropped to his knees. His antlers pierced the ground; he bellowed and fell.

He was dying, his eyes glazed with the pain-killing drug of shock; yet his muscles still flexed. His hoofs flailed at the three who were ending the hunt with slashes and blood-letting bites.

After what seemed to Miyax an eternity, the bull lay still. Amaroq tore open his side as if it were a loaf of bread and, without ceremony, fell to the feast.

Kapu and the little wolves came cautiously up to the huge animal and sniffed. They did not know what to do with the beast. It was the first one they had seen and so they wandered curiously around the kill, watching their elders. Amaroq snarled with pleasure as he ate, then licked his lips and looked at Kapu. Kapu pounced on a piece of meat and snarled, too; then he looked at Amaroq again. The leader growled and ate. Kapu growled and ate.

Miyax could not believe her good fortune—an entire caribou felled practically at her door. This was enough food to last her for months, perhaps a year. She would smoke it to make it lighter to carry, pack it, and walk to the coast. She would make it to Point Hope.

Plans racing in her head, she squatted to watch the wolves eat, measuring, as time passed, the enormous amounts they were consuming—pounds at each bite. As she saw her life-food vanishing, she decided she had better get her share while she could, and went into her house for her knife.

As she crept up toward the bull she wondered if she should come so close to the wolves that were eating. Dogs would bite people under similar conditions. But dogs would refuse to share their food with others of their kind, as the wolves were doing now, growling pleasantly and feasting in friendship.

She was inching forward, when Kapu splintered a bone with his mere baby teeth. She thought better of taking her share; instead she waited patiently for the wolves to finish.

Amaroq left the kill first, glanced her way, and disappeared into the fog. Silver and Nails departed soon after and the pups followed at their mother's heels.

"Ee-lie!" Miyax shouted and ran to the food. Suddenly Jello came out of the fog and leaped up on a leg of the kill. She drew back. Why had he not eaten with the others? She asked herself. He had not been baby-sitting. He must be in some kind of wolf disgrace, for he walked with his tail between his legs and he was not allowed to eat with the pack.

When he too had feasted and left, she walked over to the caribou and admired the mountain of food. Impulsively, she paid tribute to the spirit of the caribou by lifting her arms to the sun. Then, scoffing at herself for being such an old-fashioned Eskimo, she sharpened her man's knife on a stone and set to work.

The skin was tough and she marveled that the wolves tore it so easily. Even as she peeled it away from the flesh with her knife, she was surprised how difficult it was to cut and handle, but she worked diligently, for the pelt was almost as valuable as the meat. Hours and hours later, the last bit of hide came free and she flopped on her back to rest.

"Such hard work!" she gasped aloud. "No wonder this job is given to Eskimo men and boys." With a sigh she got to her feet, dragged the skin to her house, and laid it out to dry. Scraping and cleaning the skin was something she knew more about, for that was a woman's job, but she was too busy to do that now. It was time to carve and eat! She cut open the belly and lifted out the warm liver, the "candy" of her people. With a deft twist of the ulo, she cut off a slice and savored each bite of this, the most nourishing part of the animal. So rich is the liver that most of it is presented to the women and girls, an ancient custom with wisdom at its core—since women give birth to babies, they need the iron and blood of the liver.

All during the wolf sleep Miyax stayed up, cutting off strips of caribou and hanging them over the fire. As she worked, a song came to mind.

> *Amaroq, wolf, my friend,*
> *You are my adopted father.*
> *My feet shall run because of you.*
> *My heart shall beat because of you.*
> *And I shall love because of you.*

She stood up, peeked around the heave, and added, "But not Daniel. I'm a wolf now, and wolves love leaders."

The umbrella of fog lifted and Miyax ran up the side of her frost heave to see how her family was. They were sleeping peacefully—all but Amaroq. He shot her a glance, lifted his lips, and spoke with his teeth.

"Oh, all right. Ee-lie, Ee-lie." Miyax got down on all fours. "But how am I going to follow you if you won't let me walk? I am me, your two-legged pup." She stood up. Amaroq lifted his eyebrows, but did not reprimand her. He seemed to understand she could not change. His tail banged once and he went back to sleep.

Hunts CAME AND WENT. The smoke curled up from Miyax's fire, and caribou strips shrank and dried. One night she watched the dipping sun, trying to guess the date. It must be the second week of August, for the sun sat almost on the rim of the earth.

The wolves had no doubt about the date; they were using a calendar set by the pups, and today was the second day of exploration. Yesterday, Silver had taken them out on the tundra to chase caribou and now they were bouncing around her, ready to go again. Kapu dashed off a few steps, came back, and spun in a circle. Silver finally gave the signal to go, and led him and the others down the hill and out behind the pond.

Miyax watched them trot off to learn about the scent of caribou and the joy of chasing foxes. She wished she could learn such things, too. Shouldering her pack, she wandered through the grasses in search of fuel, a much less exciting assignment. About an hour later she saw Silver and the pups and paused to watch them chase a lively young buck. Kapu ran with a skill that almost matched his mother's. Miyax waved to them and started home.

As she rounded the pond she squinted at the sun again, for it had not climbed up the sky but was still sitting on the horizon. This worried her; it was later than she thought. Autumn was almost here. A glance across the barrens reaffirmed this. The flowers were gone; the birds flocked in great clouds, and among them were eider and old squaw ducks that kept to the rivers and beaches except when they migrated south. Finally, she saw, like hundreds of huge black fingers, the antlers of the caribou beyond the turn of the horizon. They were moving to their wintering ground ahead of the deep freeze and the snow.

She wondered why they passed so close to their enemies the wolves, then recalled how swiftly they could run. The young and the healthy ones did not fear the wolves, and the sick and the old were doomed in winter. Her caribou had been so infested with the larvae of nose flies it had not been able to eat. A weakling, it had become food to give strength both to her and to the wolves.

After storing her fuel she returned to the kill to cut off more strips to smoke. As she approached she saw Jello there and she felt uneasy, for the wolves had not touched the caribou since the night they had felled it. She liked to think they had given it to her.

Jello snarled. "That's not nice," she said. "Go away!" He growled fiercely and she realized she had not seen him with the rest of the pack for several sleeps. He was not even baby-sitting now, for the pups went out with their mother at night. She shouted again, for she needed every bite of that meat. Hearing anger in her voice he stood up, the hairs on his back rising menacingly. She backed away.

Hurrying to camp, she got out her man's knife and began to dig. Every Eskimo family had a deep cellar in the permafrost into which they put game. So cold is the ground that huge whales and caribou freeze overnight, preserved for the months to come. Miyax dug to the frost line, then whacked at the ice until, many hours later, she had chopped three feet into it. This was not the eighteen-foot-deep cellar of her mother-in-law, but perhaps it would keep the rest of her food from Jello. Cautiously she went back to the kill. Jello was gone. Working swiftly, she chopped off the best pieces and dragged them to her refrigerator. Then she covered the hole with a large slab of sod.

She was heating a pot of stew when Kapu came around the hill with a bone in his mouth. Miyax laughed at the sight, for although he ran like an adult on the tundra, he was still a puppy with games on his mind. She lifted a chunk of cooked meat from the pot and held it out to her brother.

"It's good," she said. "Try some Eskimo food." Kapu sniffed the meat, gulped, licked his jaws, and whined for more. She gave him a second bite; then Silver came and he trotted obediently home. A few minutes later he was back for another bite.

"Maybe you'll learn to like it so much, you'll travel with me," she said, and threw him another chunk of meat. "That would be nice, for I will be lonely without you." Kapu suddenly looked at her and pressed back his ears. She understood his problem instantly and danced lightly from one foot to the other.

"It's all right, Kapu," she said. "Amaroq has agreed that I can go on two feet. I am, after all, a person."

Unnumbered evenings later, when most of the meat was smoked, Miyax decided she had time to make herself a new mitten. She cut off a piece of the new caribou hide and was scraping it clean of fur when a snowstorm of cotton-grass seeds blew past her face. "Autumn," she whispered and scraped faster. She saw several birds on the sedges. They were twisting and turning and pointing their beaks toward the sun as they took their readings and plotted their courses south.

With a start, Miyax noticed the sun. It was halfway below the horizon. Shading her eyes, she watched it disappear completely. The sky turned navy blue, the clouds turned bright yellow, and twilight was upon the land. The sun had set. In a few weeks the land would be white with snow and in three months the long Arctic night that lasted for sixty-six days would darken the top of the world. She tore a fiber from the skin, threaded her needle, and began to stitch the mitten.

About an hour later, the sun arose and marked the date for Miyax. It was August twenty-fourth, the day the *North Star* reached Barrow. Of this she was sure, for on that day the sun lingered below the horizon for about one hour. After that, the nights lengthened rapidly until November twenty-first, when the sun disappeared for the winter.

In bed that evening, Miyax's spirit was stirred by the seeding grass and the restless birds and she could not sleep. She got up, stored some of the smoked meat in her pack, spread the rest in the sun to pack later, and hurried out to the caribou hide. She scraped all the fat from it and stuffed it in the bladder she had saved. The fat was excellent fuel, and gave light when burned. Finally she crept to her cellar for the rest of the meat and found Jello digging through the lid of sod.

"No!" she screamed. He snarled and came toward her. There was nothing left to do but assert her authority. She rose to her feet and tapped the top of his nose with her man's knife. With that, he stuck his tail between his legs and slunk swiftly away, while Miyax stood still, surprised by the power she felt. The knife made her a predator, and a dangerous one.

Clutching her food, she ran home, banked the fire, and put the last of the meat on the coals. She was about to go to bed when Kapu bounced down her heave, leaped over her house, and landed silently by her side.

"Oh, wow!" she said. "I'm so glad to see you. Jello scares me to death these days." She reached into her pot for a piece of cooked meat for him and this time he ate from her fingers. Then he spanked the ground to play. Picking up a scrap from the mitten, she swung it around her head. Kapu leaped and snatched it so easily that she was startled. He was quick and powerful, an adult not a pup. She hesitated to chase him, and he bounded up the heave and dashed away.

The next morning when she went out to soften the hide by pounding and chewing it, she saw two bright eyes peering at her from behind the antlers, about all that was left of her caribou. The eyes belonged to an Arctic fox and she walked toward him upright to scare him away. He continued to gnaw the bones.

"Things are tough, eh, little fox?" she whispered. "I cannot drive you away from the food." At the sound of her voice, however, his ears twisted, his tail drooped, and he departed like a leaf in the wind. The fox's brown fur of summer was splotched with white patches, reminding Miyax again that winter was coming, for the fur of the fox changes each season to match the color of the land. He would soon be white, like the snow.

Before sundown the temperature dropped and Miyax crawled into her sleeping skin early. Hardly had she snuggled down in her furs than a wolf howled to the south.

"I am here!" Amaroq answered with a bark, and the distant wolf said something else—she did not know what. Then each pack counted off and when the totals were in, Miyax's wolves yipped among themselves as if discussing the tundra news—a pack of twelve wolves to the north. So wild had their voices been that Miyax crept to her door to call Kapu to come and ease her fears. She started with surprise. There by her pond was Amaroq. The wind was blowing his fur and his tribe was gathered around him, biting his chin, kissing his cheeks. With a sudden sprint he sped into the green shadows of sunrise and one by one his family fell in behind, according to their status in the pack. Nails ran second, then Silver, Kapu, Sister, Zit, Zat, Zing, and finally, far behind came Jello.

Miyax at last was sure of what had happened to Jello. He was low man on the totem pole, the bottom of the ladder. She recalled the day Amaroq had put him down and forced him to surrender, the many times Silver had made him go back and sit with the pups, and the times that Kapu had ignored his calls to come home to the den. He was indeed a lowly wolf—a poor spirit, with fears and without friends.

Scrambling to her feet she watched the pack run along the horizon, a flowing line of magnificent beasts, all cooperating for the sake of each other, all wholly content—except Jello. He ran head down, low to the ground—in the manner of the lone wolf.

"That is not good," she said aloud.

An Arctic tern skimmed low and she jumped to her feet, for it was flying with a determination that she had not seen in the birds all summer. Its white wings cut a flashing V against the indigo sky as it moved due south across the tundra. There was no doubt in her mind what that steady flight meant—the migration was on.

"Good-bye!" she called sadly. "Good-bye."

Another tern passed overhead, then another, and another. Miyax walked to the fireplace and threw on more fuel.

Amaroq howled in the distance, his royal voice ringing out in a firm command. Somehow, she felt, he was calling her. But she could not go on this hunt. She must finish smoking every morsel of meat. Hurriedly she picked up her markers and started off for more fuel.

Several hours later, her tights bulging with caribou chips, she saw the wolves again. Amaroq, Nails, and Silver were testing the herd and Kapu was pouncing and bouncing. She knew what that meant; the hour of the lemmings was returning. Of this she was sure; she had often seen the dogs, foxes, and children hop and jump after lemmings in this same laughable way.

"I'm glad to know that," she called to her friend, and hurried back to the fire.

As the chips glowed red, Miyax saw another Arctic tern flying the same route as the others. Quickly she drew its course across the mark on the ground to Fairbanks; then, peeling off a strip of sinew, she stood in the center of the X and held the ends of the thread in both hands. When one arm was pointing to the coast and the other was pointing in the direction the bird was taking, she cut off the remainder of the strip.

"There," she said, "I have a compass. I can't take the stones with me, but every time a tern flies over, I can line up one arm with him, stretch the sinew out, and my other hand will point to the coast and Point Barrow."

That night she unzipped a small pocket in her pack and took out a battered letter from Amy.

> . . . And when you get to San Francisco, we will buy you summer dresses, and because you like curls, we'll curl your hair. Then we'll ride the trolley to the theater and sit on velvet seats.
>
> Mom says you can have the pink bedroom that looks over the garden and down on the bay and the Golden Gate Bridge.
>
> When are you coming to San Francisco?
>
> Your pen pal,
> Amy

"The theater," she whispered, "and the Golden Gate Bridge." That night she slept with the letter under her cheek.

In the evening of the following day Miyax hastily put on her clothes and crawled up the frost heave. Like a good puppy she got down on her stomach.

"Amaroq," she called. "I'm ready to go when you are!"

The wind blew across the wolf den, shattering the heads of the cotton grass and shooting their seedlets south with the birds. No one answered. The wolves were gone.

# Part II

# Miyax, the Girl

THE WIND, THE EMPTY SKY, the deserted earth—Miyax had felt the bleakness of being left behind once before.

She could not remember her mother very well, for Miyax was scarcely four when she died, but she did remember the day of her death. The wind was screaming wild high notes and hurling ice-filled waves against the beach. Kapugen was holding her hand and they were walking. When she stumbled he put her on his shoulders, and high above the beach she saw thousands of birds diving toward the sea. The jaegers screamed and the sandpipers cried. The feathered horns of the comical puffins drooped low, and Kapugen told her they seemed to be grieving with him.

She saw this, but she was not sad. She was divinely happy going somewhere alone with Kapugen. Occasionally he climbed the cliffs and brought her eggs to eat; occasionally he took her in his arms and leaned against a rock. She slept at times in the warmth of his big seal-skin parka. Then they walked on. She did not know how far.

Later, Kapugen's Aunt Martha told her that he had lost his mind the day her mother died. He had grabbed Miyax up and walked out of his fine house in Mekoryuk. He had left his important job as manager of the reindeer herd, and he had left all his possessions.

"He walked you all the way to seal camp," Martha told her. "And he never did anything good after that."

To Miyax the years at seal camp were infinitely good. The scenes and events were beautiful color spots in her memory. There was Kapugen's little house of driftwood, not far from the beach. It was rosy-gray on the outside. Inside, it was gold-brown. Walrus tusks gleamed and drums, harpoons, and man's knives decorated the walls. The sealskin kayak beside the door glowed as if the moon had been stretched across it and its graceful ribs shone black. Dark gold and soft brown were the old men who sat around Kapugen's camp stove and talked to him by day and night.

The ocean was green and white, and was rimmed by fur, for she saw it through Kapugen's hood as she rode to sea with him on his back inside the parka. Through this frame she saw the soft eyes of the seals on the ice. Kapugen's back would grow taut as he lifted his arms and fired his gun. Then the ice would turn red.

The celebration of the Bladder Feast was many colors—black, blue, purple, fire-red; but Kapugen's hand around hers was rose-colored and that was the color of her memory of the Feast. A shaman, an old priestess whom everyone called "the bent woman," danced. Her face was streaked with black soot. When she finally bowed, a fiery spirit came out of the dark wearing a huge mask that jingled and terrified Miyax. Once, in sheer bravery, she peeked up under a mask and saw that the dancer was not a spirit at all but Naka, Kapugen's serious partner. She whispered his name and he laughed, took off his mask, and sat down beside Kapugen. They talked and the old men joined them. Later that day Kapugen blew up seal bladders and he and the old men carried them out on the ice. There they dropped them into the sea, while Miyax watched and listened to their songs. When she came back to camp the bent women told her that the men had returned the bladders to the seals.

"Bladders hold the spirit of the animals," she said. "Now the spirits can enter the bodies of the newborn seals and keep them safe until we harvest them again." That night the bent women seemed all violet-colored as she tied a piece of seal fur and blubber to Miyax's belt. "It's an i'noGo tied," she said. "It's a nice little spirit for you."

Another memory was flickering-yellow—it was of the old men beating their drums around Kapugen's stove. She saw them through a scarf of tiny crystals that was her breath on the cold night air inside the house.

Naka and Kapugen were on their hands and knees, prancing lightly, moving swiftly. When Naka tapped Kapugen's chin with his head, Kapugen rose to his knees. He threw back his head, then rocked back on his heels. Naka sat up and together they sang the song of the wolves. When the dance was over the old men cheered and beat their paddle-like drums.

"You are wolves, you are real wolves," they had cried.

After that Kapugen told her about the wolves he had known on the mainland when he went to high school in Nome. He and his joking partner would hunt the wilderness for months, calling to the wolves, speaking their language to ask where the game was. When they were successful, they returned to Nome with sled-loads of Caribou.

"Wolves are brotherly," he said. "They love each other, and if you learn to speak to them, they will love you too."

He told her that the birds and animals all had languages and if you listened and watched them you could learn about their enemies, where their food lay, and when big storms were coming.

A silver memory was the day when the sun came over the horizon for the first time in winter. She was at the beach, close to Kapugen, helping him haul in a huge gleaming net. In it was a beautiful white whale. Out of sight on the other side of the whale, she could hear the old men as they cheered this gift from the sea.

The whale was a mountain so high she could not see the cliffs beyond, only the sunlit clouds. Kapugen's huge, black, frostbitten hand seemed so small as it touched the great body of the whale.

Not far away the bent woman was dancing and gathering invisible things from the air. Miyax was frightened but Kapugen explained that she was putting the spirit of the whale in her i'noGo tied.

"She will return it to the sea and the whales," he said.

Walking the tundra with Kapugen was all laughter and fun. He would hail the blue sky and shout out his praise for the grasses and bushes. On these trips they ate salmon berries, then lay in the sun watching the birds. Sometimes Kapugen would whistle sandpiper songs and the birds would dip down to see which of their members had gotten lost in the grass. When they saw him and darted away, Kapugen would laugh.

Fishing with Kapugen was murky-tan in her memory, for they would wade out into the river mouth where the stone weirs were built and drive the fish into nets between the walls. Kapugen would spear them or grab them in his hand and throw them to the men in the wooden boats. Occasionally he skimmed after the biggest cod and halibut in his Kayak and he would whoop with joy when he caught one and would hold it above his head. It gleamed as it twisted in the sun.

Summers at seal camp were not as beautiful to Miyax as the autumns and winters, for during this season many families from Mekoryuk came to Nash Harbor to hunt and fish and Kapugen was busy. Sometimes he helped people set nets; sometimes he scouted the ocean in his kayak as he searched for seal colonies.

During these hours Miyax was left with the other children on the beach. She played tag and grass ball with them and she pried prickly sea urchins off the rocks, to eat the sweet meat inside. Often she dug for clams and when Kapugen returned he would crack them open and smack his lips as he swallowed them whole.

The Eskimos from Mekoryuk spoke English almost all the time. They called her father Charlie Edward and Miyax was Julie, for they all had two names, Eskimo and English. Her mother had also called her Julie, so she did not mind her summer name until one day when Kapugen called her that. She stomped her foot and told him her name was Miyax. "I am Eskimo, not a gussak!" she had said, and he tossed her into the air and hugged her to him.

"Yes, you are Eskimo," he had said. "And never forget it. We live as no other people can, for we truly understand the earth."

But winters always returned. Blizzards came and the temperatures dropped to thirty and forty below zero, and those who stayed at hunting camp spoke only in Eskimo and did only Eskimo things. They scraped hides, mended boots, made boats, and carved walrus tusks. In the evenings Kapugen sang and danced with the old men, and all of their songs and dances were about the sea and the land and the creatures that dwelled there.

One year, probably in September, for the canvas tents were down and the campground was almost empty, Kapugen came into the house with a sealskin. It was a harbor seal, but had so few spots that it was a rare prize.

"We must make you a new coat," he had said. "You are getting big. Since your mother is not here to help us, I will do her work. Now watch and learn."

The skin was metallic silver-gold and so beautiful that even the velveteen parkas of the children from Mekoryuk paled by comparison. Miyax stroked it lovingly as Kapugen lay her old coat upon it and began to cut a larger one. As he worked he hummed, and she made up words about the seal who wanted to be a coat. Presently they became aware of the distant throb of a motorboat. The sound grew louder, then shut off at the beach. Footsteps crunched, the cold air rushed in the door, and there was Martha, Kapugen's aunt. She was thin and her face was pinched. Miyax disliked her immediately, but was spared the necessity of speaking nicely to her, for Martha had words only for Kapugen.

She talked swiftly in English, which Miyax barely understood, and she was angry and upset. Martha shook her finger at Kapugen and glanced at Miyax from time to time. The two were arguing very loudly when Martha pulled a sheet of paper from her pocket and showed it to Kapugen.

"No!" he shouted.

"We'll see!" Martha screamed, turned around, and went toward the boat where a white man waited. Kapugen followed her and stood by the boat, talking to the man for a long time.

The next morning Miyax was awakened as Kapugen lifted her up in his arms and held her close. Gently he pushed the hair out of her eyes and, speaking softly in Eskimo, told her she was going to live with Aunt Martha.

"There's a law that says you must go to school . . . and I guess you should. You are nine years old. And I must go to war. The government is fighting somewhere."

Miyax grabbed him around the neck, but did not protest. It never occurred to her that anything that Kapugen decided was not absolutely perfect. She whimpered however.

"Listen closely," he said. "If anything happens to me, and if you are unhappy, when you are thirteen you can leave Aunt Martha by marrying Daniel, Naka's son. Naka is going to Barrow on the Arctic Ocean. I shall make arrangements with him. He is like me, an old-time Eskimo who likes our traditions. He will agree."

Miyax listened carefully, then he put her down and hastily packed her bladder-bag, wrapped her in an oilskin against the wild spray of the sea, and carried her to the boat. She sat down beside Martha and stared bravely at Kapugen. The motor started and Kapugen looked at her until the boat moved, then he turned his back and walked quickly away. The launch sped up a huge wave, slammed down into a foaming trough, and Kapugen was no longer visible.

With that Miyax became Julie. She was given a cot near the door in Martha's little house and was soon walking to school in the darkness. She liked to learn the printed English words in the books, and so a month passed rather happily.

One morning when the air was cold and the puddles around the house were solid ice, an old man from seal camp arrived at the door.

He spoke softly to Martha, then pulled his hood tightly around his face and went away. Martha came to Miyax's bed.

"Your father," she said, "went seal hunting in that ridiculous kayak. He has been gone a month this day. He will not be back. Bits of his kayak washed up on the shore." Martha stumped to the fire and turned her back.

Julie ran out of the house into the dark morning. She darted past the store, the reindeer-packing house, the church. She did not stop until she came to the beach. There she crouched among the oil drums and looked out on the sea.

The wind blew across the water, shattering the tips of the waves and shooting ice-sparklets north with the storm. "Kapugen!" she called. No one answered. Kapugen was gone. The earth was empty and bleak.

GRADUALLY JULIE PUSHED KAPUGEN out of her heart and accepted the people of Mekoryuk. The many years in seal camp alone with Kapugen had been dear and wonderful, but she realized now that she had lived a strange life. The girls her age could speak and write English and they knew the names of presidents, astronauts, and radio and movie personalities who lived below the top of the world. Maybe the Europeans once thought the earth was flat, but the Eskimos always knew it was round. One only needed to look at the earth's relatives, the sun and the moon, to know that.

One day as she walked home across the snowy town she caught up with her schoolmates, Judith and Rose. Their boots squeaked in the cold and their voices sounded far away, for the temperature was far below zero. Judith invited her into the house and the three of them huddled close to the oil stove. Judith and Rose chatted, but Julie's eyes wandered around the room and she saw for the first time a gas cooking stove, a couch, framed pictures on the wall, and curtains of cotton print. Then Judith took her into her own room and she beheld a bed with a headboard, a table, and a reading lamp. On the table lay a little chain on which hung a dog, a hat, a boat. This she was glad to see—something familiar.

"What a lovely i'noGo tied!" Julie said politely.

"A what?" asked Judith. Julie repeated the Eskimo word for the house of the spirits.

Judith snickered. "That's a charm bracelet," she said. Rose giggled and both laughed derisively. Julie felt the blood rush to her face as she met, for the first but not the last time, the new attitudes of the Americanized Eskimos. She had much to learn besides reading. That night she threw her i'noGo tied away.

English and math came easily to her, and by the end of the year Julie was reading and writing. That summer she worked at the mission beside the church sweeping the floor and greeting the visitors from the lower states who came to see real Eskimos. She read the encyclopedia when there was nothing else to do.

The next year Julie worked at the hospital on weekends. After school she cut out dresses in the domestic science room and sewed them on electric machines. She bobbed her hair and put it in rollers to make the ends curl.

One Sunday, as she was coming home from the hospital, a jeep pulled up beside her and a gussak hailed her. He leaned on the steering wheel, a warm smile on his face.

"I'm Mr. Pollock. I own stock in the Reindeer Corporation here on the island," he said. "And I have a daughter your age. The last thing she asked me before I left San Francisco was to find a girl in the town of Mekoryuk on Nunivak Island and ask if she would like to exchange letters. How about being her pen pal?"

Julie needed no explanation for that term. Many letters came into the mission from children in the States who wanted to write letters. She had never done so before, but now she was ready.

"I would like that," she answered.

"My daughter's name is Amy," he said, taking a letter from his inside pocket. "She told me to give this to the nicest girl I could find— and that's you, with your twinkling eyes and rosy cheeks."

Julie smiled and slowly took the extended letter, then skipped off to open it in the privacy of the mission library. She was enchanted by what she read:

*Hello, my new friend,*

*I am Amy Pollack and I have blue eyes and brown hair. Next month I will be twelve years old, and I hope I'll be five feet tall by then. I have a quarter of an inch to go. I wear a size nine dress and a size six shoe, which my mother finds embarrassingly big. Frankly, I like my big feet. They get me up and down the steep hills of San*

Francisco and shoot me through the water like a frog when I swim. I am in the eighth grade and am studying French. I hate it, but would like to learn Eskimo. My father goes to Alaska often and has taught me a few words. They are pretty words that sound like bells, but I can't spell them. Can you? How do you spell the word for "daylight?" Quaq?

I take dancing lessons, which I love, and I also like to play baseball with the kids that live on our hill. When I grow up I think I'll be a dancer, but it is an awful lot of work. One of the dancers at the San Francisco Opera House said so, so maybe I'll be a schoolteacher like my aunt and have the whole summer off.

Last month at school we saw your island on a television show. It was so beautiful, with the birds flying over it and the flowers blooming on its hills, that I wanted to write to someone who lives there, a girl like me.

Here is a picture of my house. That is me standing on one foot on the patio wall. Please write soon.

Your new friend,<br>Amy

P.S. When are you coming to live with us in San Francisco?

Julie folded the letter and whispered to herself: "Daylight is spelled A-M-Y."

The wonders of Mekoryuk dimmed as weekly letters from Amy arrived. Julie learned about television, sports cars, blue jeans, bikinis, hero sandwiches, and wall-to-wall carpeting in the high school Amy would soon be attending. Mekoryuk had no high school. The Eskimo children of the more prosperous families were sent to the mainland for further schooling, something which Aunt Martha could not afford. But, she thought, if she married Daniel, perhaps Naka could send her to school.

As the winter passed, Martha became irritated with her. She nagged Julie for wearing her hair short, and complained about Judith. "She's disrespectful of her parents," she snapped. "And she's bad." That's all she would say except, "The old ways are best."

After that Martha gave her chores to do on weekends and refused to let her attend the movies with her friends. The winter nights in the dark little house became nightmares. Julie waited for letters from Amy and the call from Naka.

The call came suddenly. One morning in June as Julie was dressing to go to the store, the head of the Indian Affairs in Mekoryuk appeared at the door. He explained that Naka had written, requesting Julie to come to Barrow and marry his son.

"You are now thirteen," the man said, "and I have in my files an agreement for this arrangement signed by Kapugen and Naka." Martha sputtered and whispered in her ear that she could say no if she wanted to.

"The old ways are best," Julie said, and Martha could not protest.

The next day transportation was arranged for her by the Bureau of Indian Affairs and Julie packed her few possessions in a moosehide bag and walked to the airport with Martha. The old lady dragged behind, taking slow steps, and by the time they reached the airport she was limping.

"What shall I do when I'm too crippled to get out of bed?" she said angrily. Julie was about to remind her how strong her legs had been a few hours ago, but had time to say no more than good-bye. The pilot himself escorted her up the steps into the gleaming cabin and showed her how to fasten her seat belt.

Cautiously she looked at the upholstery, the overhead lights, the open door to the pilot's cabin—then she closed her eyes. She was afraid the plane could not really fly. The engines roared, the ship moved, and minutes later she opened her eyes to see the houses of Nunivak shrink to specks and the island grow smaller and smaller. When it was but a jewel in the sea, she touched her seat and her armrest and stared down at herself.

"I'm sitting in the sky!" she said to the man beside her. He winked and she pressed her head against the window. She was an eagle seeking out new pinnacles. After a long time she relaxed and her wonder at the miraculous airship changed to curiosity.

"What makes us stay up here?" she asked the man.

"That's not a good question," he said, and she lapsed into silence. The plane landed in Anchorage, then Fairbanks. Here she was put on another plane, a smaller one—the only one that flew to remote Barrow.

Rugged mountain passes and valleys passed below her; the trees became smaller and more scarce, then disappeared entirely as the craft shot out over the North Slope and the pilot announced that they were crossing the Arctic Circle. The gussaks cheered and opened bottles to toast the mythical line, but hardly had they taken sips than the windows became white and the plane was bumping along through a summer fog.

They made wide circles over Barrow for an hour and a half before the pilot announced they would try once more to find an opening in the fog, then head back to Fairbanks. Julie had her nose pressed tightly to the window, for she could see the long threads that spoke of a clearing. Suddenly Barrow appeared below, its houses huddled against the ice-piled shore like a cluster of lonely birds.

As the plane began its descent into Barrow, Julie could see in the distance the towers of the Distant Early Warning System that marked the presence of the military in Barrow, and a narrow road along the coast that led to a group of buildings. The pilot announced that they belonged to the Navy and the University of Alaska. "The Arctic Research Laboratory," he said, "where scientists study the Arctic. People from all over the world come here to investigate the top of the world. We now know a lot about living in the cold."

The wheels struck the runway and the plane pulled up by a small wooden house on the tundra, the terminal building. For a moment Julie had misgivings about her fate; then the stewardess brought her coat and escorted her to the door. She looked down at two people she knew must be Naka and his wife, Nusan. Daniel was hiding behind them. Slowly Julie walked down the steps, crossed the stretch of macadam and took Naka's hand. He was dressed in a Navy Arctic field jacket and his eyes were dark and smiling. She remembered those eyes from her color wheel of memories and she felt better.

Nusan was dressed in a kuspuck trimmed with Japanese lace flowers and she was smiling at Julie. They had not met before. Nusan had never gone to seal camp.

Then Julie saw Daniel. She knew from his grin and dull eyes that something was wrong with him. Nusan must have seen the disappointment that flashed over her face, for she put her arm around Julie.

"Daniel has a few problems," she said quickly. "But he's a very good boy, and he's a good worker. He cleans the animal cages at the research lab. He will be like a brother to you."

With those words Julie relaxed, and pushed him out of her mind. He would just be a brother. That was fine. She looked at the little houses surrounded by boats, oil drums, tires, buckets, broken cars, and rags and bags, and happily followed her new parents home.

The very next day, however, to Julie's surprise, there was a wedding. The minister came to Naka's house with two strangers and Nusan took Julie into the kitchen and gave her a beautiful sealskin suit. She helped her to dress. Daniel put on a dark blue shirt and gussak pants. They were told to stand in the doorway between the living room and kitchen, and the minister began to read. Daniel grasped her hand. His was as clammy with anxiety as hers. She stared at the floor wondering if Kapugen had known that Daniel was dull. She would not believe he did.

When the reading was over Daniel escaped to the kitchen and sat on his bed. He began to tinker with a radio and mumble to himself. Naka walked outside with the minister and the two strangers, and Nusan sat down at her sewing machine.

"I've got to finish these boots for a tourist," she said. "Make yourself at home." The sewing machine hummed and the radio droned on. Julie stepped outside and sat down on an oil drum. The streets were hushed for it was the rest hour. She did not know how long she sat in quiet terror, but it was a long time. Presently a little girl came around a rusted ship's engine, pulling a smaller girl by the hand.

"Come on," she ordered the reluctant child. "It's time for the blanket toss." As they hurried along, other children gathered from all directions and clustered in front of the community house. Several men unfolded a huge skin. Eskimos and tourists took hold of it. A child got in the center, bounced, and then was flipped twenty feet up in the air, like a toy rocket. Giggling, the child kicked her feet as if she were running, and came gracefully down.

Julie looked away. Snow buntings whirled around the house, an Arctic tern darted over the ocean, and the waves lapped the ice that was piled high on the shore. She was desperately homesick for Mekoryuk. She dropped her head on her knees.

"Julie?" a tall girl tapped her arm. "I'm Pearl Norton, Pani NalaGan." She began speaking in Iñupiat. Julie shook her head. She spoke Yupik.

"We'd better use English," she said. Pearl nodded and laughed.

"I said, 'Let's go to the quonset.'" Julie jumped to her feet and followed Pearl around a broken box, over a battered auto door, and into an alley. In silence they passed the wooden hotel, where a tourist was huddled on the porch out of the wind; then they stepped onto the main street, where the stores stood. Crossing the street they entered an enormous quonset hut. When Julie's eyes had adjusted to the dim light she could see a dozen or more young men and girls, some in blue jeans and field jackets, some in kuspucks and parkas. They were seated at tables or leaning against pinball machines as they listened to rock and roll music. Pearl bought a Coke, got two straws, and they sat down at a table near the door.

"I know how you feel, Julie. I was married last year," Pearl began. "Don't pay any attention to it. No one does. All you have to do is leave the house or run away and everything's forgotten. Most of these arrangements are for convenience. I'm sure you are here to help Nusan make parkas and mittens for the tourists." Pearl leaned back. "Even in the old days they didn't make kids stick with these marriages if they didn't like each other. They just drifted apart."

Julie listened, her head swimming in confusion . . . Daniel, marriage, parkas, tourists, jukeboxes, pinball machines . . . divorce.

"I must go," Julie said. "Can I talk to you again?"

"I'll meet you here tomorrow. All the kids come here to have fun."

Daniel was gone when Julie stepped into the kitchen and nervously glanced around.

"Do you know how to sew?" Nusan yelled from the floor where she was cutting a short length of rabbit fur.

"A little," Julie answered as she unzipped her coat and folded it carefully.

"You shall know a lot when I'm through with you," Nusan replied and pointed to a large box in the corner. "Yard goods and rickrack. We have to make thirty parkas for the airlines by the end of the month. They lend them to the tourists who come here. None of them know how to dress. They'd freeze without parkas." Nusan threaded a needle and whipped the rabbit fur onto the top of a mukluk. She glanced up at Julie.

"You'll do nicely," she said. "You're smart and you're pretty."

Julie saw little of Daniel that summer and even less of him after school started. And so, by October she was beginning to enjoy her new home. She cooked and sewed for Nusan, studied at night, and had a few hours in the afternoon when she met Pearl at the quonset.

As the months passed, the letters from Amy became the most

important thing in Julie's life and the house in San Francisco grew more real than the house in Barrow. She knew each flower on the hill where Amy's house stood, each brick in the wall around the garden, and each tall blowing tree. She also knew the curls in the wrought-iron gate, and how many steps led up to the big front door; she could almost see the black-and-white tile on the floor of the foyer. If she closed her eyes she could imagine the arched doorway, the Persian rug on the living-room floor, the yellow chairs and the huge window that looked over the bay. Radios, lamps, coffee tables—all these she could see. And if she shut her eyes tight, she could feel Amy's hand in her hand and hear Amy's big feet tap the sidewalk.

The second floor was always fun to dream about. At the top of the winding stairs four doors opened upon rooms lit with sunshine. And one was the pink room, the one that would be hers when she got to San Francisco.

DURING THE WINTER Julie came to understand Naka. At first she thought he had a very important job, for he would be gone for days, often weeks, and be very tired and angry when he came home. He slept sometimes for two days. But when the subzero weather set in, Naka stayed home, and Julie realized that he did not work at all. He drank. The more he drank the angrier he became. Sometimes he struck Nusan; more often he picked a fight with his neighbor. Finally, numbness would overcome him and he would drop on the bed like a huge limp seal and sleep for days.

When he awoke he would be pleasant again, sitting in the fur- and scrap-filled room, making moosehide masks for the summer tourist trade. He would sing the old songs of seal camp, and tell Julie about the animals that he and Kapugen had known. On those occasions, she would understand why Kapugen had loved him.

One night he struck Nusan over and over again. When she screamed and hit back, Julie ran to the quonset to look for Pearl. She was not there, but in a corner sat Russell, the young man who had been campaigning around the village, begging the Eskimos to vote "No" on requests for liquor licenses by the local restaurants.

Julie sat down. "Naka is evil again," she said. "His spirit has fled."

Russell nodded. "He, like many others, cannot tolerate alcohol. There's a man from San Francisco who does lots of business in Alaska.

He has been able to help people like Naka. He helped my father. And me," Russell added. "Now we all join together and help each other not to drink. But Naka must agree to see him. If he does I'll try to get in touch with—"

Julie leaned forward, knowing exactly what Russell was going to say. "Mr. Pollock," she whispered.

"Ee-lie. How did you know?"

The pink room in San Francisco had a new dimension.

January twenty-third was a day of celebration. Beginning about the twenty-first, the top of the world began to glow like an eclipse as the sun circled just below the horizon. The Americans began to smile and the Eskimos put away their winter games of yo-yo and darts. Excitement mounted higher and higher each day.

The morning of the twenty-third Julie and Pearl ran all the way to school, for this was the most beautiful day of the year, the day of the sunrise.

Just before noon Julie and her classmates put on their parkas and mittens and skipped out the school door in awesome silence. The gussak principal was already outside watching the southeastern sky anxiously. His face seemed to say he really did not believe the miracle would happen.

"There it is!" a little boy shouted, as a brilliant light, first green then red, exploded on the horizon. Slowly the life-giving star arose until it was round and burning red in the sky. The Eskimos lifted their arms and turned their palms to the source of all life. Slowly, without any self-consciousness, every gussak raised his arms, too. Not one person snickered at the old Eskimo tradition.

For an hour and a half the sun moved above the horizon, reminding the Eskimos that the birds and mammals would come back, that the snow would melt, and that the great ice pack that pressed against the shore would begin to retreat and set them free to hunt and fish.

Even on Nunivak there was no such wonderful day, for the sun appeared for a little while every day of the year.

"Bright sun, I missed you so," Julie whispered, and her palms felt vibrant with life.

The little house in Barrow became home as Julie fitted into Nusan's routine, and summer was upon the land before she knew it.

Tourists arrived at the hotel every day; the research lab buzzed with activity. Julie stitched, sewed, and occasionally visited Pearl and her family.

Late one evening Nusan came back from the store. "Naka's in jail," she said angrily. "I've got to go get him. Finish these maklaks." She pointed. "A man wants them tomorrow." She hurried out the door and Julie picked up the boots. She was cutting a tiny black square to sew into the intricate band at the top when the door opened and Daniel came in.

She did not look up, for she knew his routine. He would fix himself a TV dinner, open a Coke, and sit on his cot listening to the radio.

"You!" he shouted. She looked up in surprise.

"You. You're my wife."

"Daniel, what's wrong?"

"They're laughing at me. That's what's wrong. They say, 'Ha ha. Dumb Daniel. He's got a wife and he can't mate her. Ha.'"

He pulled her to her feet and pressed his lips against her mouth. She pulled away.

"We don't have to," she cried.

"They're laughin'," he repeated, and tore her dress from her shoulders. She clutched it and pulled away. Daniel grew angry. He tripped her and followed her to the floor. His lips curled back and his tongue touched her mouth. Crushing her with his body, he twisted her down on the floor. He was as frightened as she.

The room spun, and grew blurry. Daniel cursed, kicked violently, and lay still. Suddenly he got to his feet and ran out of the house. "Tomorrow, tomorrow I can, I can, can, can, ha ha," he bleated piteously.

Julie rolled to her stomach and vomited. Slowly she got to her feet. "When fear seizes," she whispered, "change what you are doing. You are doing something wrong."

She got her red tights from a box on the shelf, slipped into a warm shirt, and put on her wedding parka and pants. Next she opened a box under the bed and picked out a pair of warm woolen socks. Shoving her feet into her boots she laced and knotted them. Daniel's old pack was under his cot. She got that, then opened a cardboard box by the stove and took out her man's knife and ulo which she had brought from Nunivak. Then she grabbed handfuls of wooden matches and dropped them into a moisture-proof cookie can.

She opened the door and walked calmly through the midnight

light to Pearl's house. Stealing quietly past her sleeping brothers and parents, she crept into Pearl's room.

"Pearl, I'm leaving," Julie whispered.

Almost instantly Pearl was awake. "Daniel?"

Julie nodded. "He is dumb. Everyone's teasing him."

Pearl slipped out of bed and together they crept to the kitchen. When the door was closed Pearl sat down.

"Where are you going?"

"I won't tell you. Then they won't bother you. I need food."

Pearl glanced at the shelves above the stove and pushed a box under them; she took down bread, cheeses, dried fruits, meats, and a bag of oats and sugar.

"That's fine," Julie said. "I only need enough for a week or so. But I need to borrow a sleeping skin and ground cloth. I'll mail them back when I get where I'm going."

Pearl slipped out to the shed and came back with the sleeping skin and hide.

"They're a wedding present." She smiled. "You can keep them. No one uses these old-timers."

"Some needles, please," Julie said, "and that'll be all." Stuffing the sleeping skin into her pack, she tied the caribou hide to the bottom and shouldered her load.

"Are you sure you'll be all right?" Pearl asked.

"My father was a great hunter. He taught me much. If Nusan asks where I am, tell her you saw me walking out on the ice. She won't look for me long after that."

With a sob Julie threw her arms around Pearl, then stepped out the door and closed it quietly behind her. She walked to the beach, climbed onto the ice, and looked back. No one was on the street but a single tourist who was photographing the sun in the sky. His back was to her. Julie ducked below the ice rim and made her way along it on hands and feet until she was beyond the village and out of sight of the rooftops of Barrow. Then she stood up and looked at the ocean.

"Julie is gone," she said. "I am Miyax now."

She leaped lightly up the bank and onto the tundra. Her stride opened wider and wider, for she was on her way to San Francisco.

# Part III

# Kapugen, the Hunter

THE MEMORIES VANISHED. The wind screamed *oooooooooeeeeeeeeeee*. Miyax touched the lichens on the top of her frost heave.

"Amaroq," she called again, then ran down the slope and climbed to the wolf den. The site was silent and eerie and the puppies' playground was speckled with bleached bones like tombstones in a graveyard.

She picked one up and saw that it was jagged with the marks of little teeth. With some carving, it could be made into the comb she had been wanting. Glancing around, she saw the club-like base of an antler. "A weapon," she said. "I may need it."

A snowy owl floated past, turning his head as he peered down at her curiously.

"I'll see you in San Francisco," she called. He set his eyes on some distant goal, bowed his wings, and flew southward as silently as the shadow he cast.

The wind twisted a strand of her hair, and as she stood on the wolf hill she felt the presence of the great animals she had lived with: Amaroq, Nails, Silver, Kapu. She wondered if she would ever see them again. The wind gusted; she turned and walked slowly back home, trailing her fingers on the tips of the sedges and thinking about her departure. At the top of her frost heave, she froze in her tracks. Her house was crushed in and her sleeping skins were torn and strewn over the grass. The meat she had laid out on the grass was gone. Her icebox was opened and empty.

"Ayi!" she cried. "My food! My life! I'm dead!"

Running from broken house to dumped cooking pot to icebox, she felt needles of fear move up her spine, spread into her arms, and pierce her whole body. Who had done this? What bestial creature had taken her food? She looked desperately around and saw, crouched in the reeds almost beside her, the angry Jello. His tail was swishing slowly, his ears were forward. She understood his message and stepped back. Then she knew that was wrong; she must not give in. Hand tightening on the antler club, brandishing it, growling, she flung herself upon him and bit the top of his nose. His eyes widened, his ears and body drooped, and his tail went between his legs. He groveled on his belly and came up to her smiling, head lowered humbly.

Desperate, furious, she lunged at him. Jello rolled to his back and flashed the white hair of surrender. She did not strike; she could not strike a coward.

"Jello!" she cried. "Why? Why did you do it?"

Holding him in abeyance with the antler, she glanced around the ruins of her home and took stock of the damage. All the food in the cellar and on the ground was gone, and her pack was not in sight. Brandishing her weapon, growling at Jello, she backed toward the sod house, kicked back the ruins, and saw the pack under the crushed roof. It was intact. Jello had not found the meat in it. Her mind raced. She had a little food and Kapu had told her that the lemmings were coming back. She could yet make it.

"Gnarlllllllll," she snapped at Jello and lowered her club. He rolled over, stood up and, tail between his legs, fled into the twilight.

When he was gone she stood for a long time. Finally she picked up her sleeping skin and tore a fiber from the new hide. She got out her needle and, sitting with her legs out straight in the manner of Eskimo women, began to sew.

A lemming ran across a lichen patch. She stopped working and watched the little animal add a mouthful of grass to its round nest. A movement caught her eye and she glanced up to see a least weasel washing his belly on the other side of the knoll. New white fur was splotched across his gold back. He finished his toilet, and when he sat down he disappeared under the reindeer moss. "You are tiny," she said and smiled. Another cycle was beginning. The animals who preyed on the lemmings were also coming back.

Miyax put her needle away, rolled her ground skin into a tight bundle, and tied it to the bottom of the pack. Then she got her pot and sleeping skin, her ulo and man's knife, the bones and her flowers. She packed them, tied a thong to the new caribou skin so she could drag it behind her, and lined up her pointer stones with a distant frost heave.

"It's time to go," she said and walked away, not looking back.

Many hours later she opened her pack, spread her skins, and took out a strand of smoked meat. A snowshoe hare screamed and, recognizing the cry of death, Miyax picked up her club and ran off to take the rabbit from its killer. Rounding a clump of grass she came upon an enormous wolverine, the king of the Arctic weasel family. Slowly he lifted his head.

The wolverine was built low to the ground, and his powerful front feet were almost as big as a man's hand. Utterly fearless, he looked her in the face.

"Shoooo," she said and jumped at him. He left the rabbit and came toward her. She jumped back and raised her club. He leapt lightly to the side, snarled, and sauntered away. Gingerly she snatched the hare, turned, and fled back to camp. The wolverine's fearlessness sent goose bumps up her spine. Hastily throwing the hare on the caribou skin she was dragging for just such a purpose, she walked on.

A tern floated past. She took out her sinew, held her arm under the bird, and singing aloud strode toward Point Hope.

At sunset the clouds were dark and soft-edged, like bears. They could dump a foot of snow or a sprinkle of snow. She dug a niche in the side of a heave with her man's knife, folded her ground skin into an envelope, and pushed it into the cave. With deft hands she pressed her sleeping skin into the envelope, then undressed. The fur nestled her, and when each toe and finger was warm she peered solemnly out of her den. The sky darkened, the clouds lowered, and the wind blew like a charging buck. In less than a minute she could see no more than the fur around her face. The snow had come.

Buried in her skins like an animal in its lair, Miyax wondered about Amaroq and Kapu. Would they be curled in furry balls, or would they be running joyously through the first storm of winter, following their noses to game?

When she awoke the sun was out, the sky was clear, and only a feathering of snow covered the tundra—just enough to make it winter. Before she had dressed, however, the crystals had melted—all but a few on the north sides of the slopes, that spoke of things to come.

Miyax pulled a snarl out of her hair with her fingers, then looked around. Someone was watching her. Running to the top of a low hill, she scanned the flatness. A dozen stout caribou, their white necks gleaming in the sunlight, browsed in the distance; but there was nothing else. She laughed at herself, went back to camp, and ate a piece of smoked meat. Rolling her skins and shouldering her pack, she walked to her caribou skin to pick up the leads. It was empty. Someone had taken her rabbit in the night. A wolverine, she thought; but there was not a footstep to tell which way the thief had gone.

She spun around. Again she felt as if someone were watching her. Again there was no one; there was only a large flock of terns in the sky. Taking a bearing on them with her sinew and adjusting her pack, she gave the skin-drag a yank and walked on.

All day the birds moved overhead. She walked a straight line to the ocean, for the pools had frozen and she could follow her compass without deviating.

When the eerie feeling of being watched persisted, Miyax began to wonder if the vast nothingness was driving her mad, as it did many gussaks. To occupy her mind she sang as she gathered caribou drop-pings and put them on her drag:

Amaroq, wolf, my friend,
You are my adopted father.
My feet shall run because of you.
My heart shall beat because of you.
And I shall love because of you.

That evening she stopped early, built a bright fire and cooked a stew, adding to it a sweet-leather lichen from the tundra. While the pot simmered and the steam hung above it like a gray spirit, she took out a needle and thread and mended a hole in her old mitten.

The earth trembled. She glanced up to see two of the largest caribou she had ever beheld. She could tell by the massiveness of their antlers that they were males, for those of the females are more slender and shorter. As the two ran side by side, the gleam of their headpieces told her it was the breeding season of the caribou. When the last fuzzy antler-coating of summer is rubbed off and the horns glow and shimmer, the mating season begins—a season of bellowing and short tempers.

Suddenly the lead bull circled and came toward the other. Both lowered their heads and clashed antlers with a clanging crack that sounded like a shot. Neither was hurt. They shook their heads and stepped back, tossed their antlers, and bellowed. Colliding again, they pawed the ground and then peacefully trotted away. Miyax wondered who they were fighting over, for not a female was to be seen. All the bravado and glamour seemed lost on the grass and the sky.

Nevertheless, when she had eaten she picked up her pack, tugged on her cumbersome drag, and moved on; for the thundering animals told her she was along the migration path and she did not want to camp in the middle of a caribou love nest.

Far from the herd, she stopped by a pond and made her bed. She was not sleepy, so she took out the wolf-puppy bone and, holding the ulo between her knees, carved a tooth in the comb.

Orange and purple shadows crept over the land as the sun went down that night, and Miyax crawled into her sleeping skin noting that the days were growing shorter. She felt restless like the birds and mammals, and in the middle of the night she awakened and peered out at the sky. A star twinkled in the half-lit dome—the first of the year! She smiled, sat up, and hugged her knees.

The guidepost of her ancestors, the North Star, would soon be visible and would point her way when the birds had all gone South.

Softly across the distance a wolf barked, then another. The first bark was one of inquiry, a sort of "Where are you and what are you doing?" The answer was a casual "I am here." The next call, however, was disquieting. The wolf seemed to be saying there was danger in the air. Miyax looked around to see what it might be. Then the wolf changed the subject and shifted to a joyous howl. As the others joined in she recognized the hunt song of her pack. Amaroq's rich tones rose and fell like a violin; then came the flute-like voice of Silver. Nails's voice arose, less strong than Amaroq's, bringing variation to the theme. Cupping her hands behind her ears, she listened intently. Yes, the pups were singing too, sounding very mature and grown up—until Kapu added his laugh-bark.

She listened for Jello to sound forth. He did not. The concert ended abruptly and she heard other sounds in the dimness. A lemming screamed in death, and a flock of migrating eider ducks called out their positions to each other.

Suddenly something moved. She bolted out of bed and grabbed her club. The grass crackled behind her and she spun around. Sedges bobbed to say it was only the wind.

"Ayi!" She was disgusted by her fears. She kicked a stone to change something, since she could not change what she was doing, as Kapugen advised. Feeling better, she slid back into her sleeping skin. "I guess," she said to herself, "that the sun's been up so long I've forgotten the sounds of the night." As she waited for sleep she listened to the polar wind whistle, and the dry grasses whined like the voice of the old bent lady.

"Jello!" she screamed, sitting bolt upright. He was almost beside her, his teeth bared as he growled. Then he picked up her pack and ran. She jumped out of bed and started after him, for her very life was in that pack—food, needles, knives, even her boots. The wind chilled her naked body and she stopped to collect her wits. She must act with wisdom. She must think! Her clothes, where were her clothes? They, too, were gone. No, she remembered, they were safe in the bladder bag under the caribou skin.

Quickly she pulled them out and clutched them to her chest, but they were of little comfort. She could go nowhere without boots; nor could she make new ones. Her needles and ulo, the tools of survival, were all in the pack. Shivering, she slid into bed and cried. A tear fell on the grass and froze solid.

"My tombstone."

She lay very still wondering how long it would take for life to leave her.

When she opened her eyes it was daylight and the warm yellow of the land gave her hope. She could eat her caribou skin if she had to. Rolling to her stomach, she smelled something sweet and recognized the scent of wolf urine. It had been dropped at the edge of her bag and was frozen but fresh. Someone had greeted her during the night. It could not have been Jello for the scent did not have the bitter odor of an angry and desolate wolf. Furthermore, it was sparsely given, not the dousing given to hostile objects. It must have been Amaroq. She sniffed again but her nose was not sensitive enough to read the other messages in the urine that meant "all is well." Yet its light and loving scent gave her a sense of security and she smiled at the sun, dressed, and put her mind to inventing boots.

Wrapping the drag around one foot and her sleeping skin around the other, she clomped awkwardly through the grass in a wider and wider circle hoping that Jello, having eaten her meat, would have abandoned the pack. She did not care about the food anymore. Her ulo and needles and matches were more important to find. With them she could make shoes, hunt, and cook. She marveled at how valuable these simple things were, how beautiful and precious. With them she could make a home, a larder, a sled, and clothes. And the cold air was equally precious. With it she could, like her father, freeze leather and sinew into sleds, spears, and harpoons. She would not die here if she could find her ulo and needles.

As she carefully searched the ground she began to think about seal camp. The old Eskimos were scientists too. By using plants, animals, and temperature, they had changed the harsh Arctic into a home, a feat as incredible as sending rockets to the moon. She smiled. The people at seal camp had not been as outdated and old-fashioned as she had been led to believe. No, on the contrary, they had been wise. They had adjusted to nature instead of to man-made gadgets.

"Ayi!" she gasped. On the side of a ground swell lay Jello, his body torn in bloody shreds, his face contorted. Beside him lay her backpack!

Instantly she knew what had happened; Amaroq had turned on him. Once Kapugen had told her that some wolves had tolerated a lone wolf until the day he stole meat from the pups. With that, the leader gave a signal and his pack turned, struck, and tore the lone wolf to pieces. "There is no room in the wolf society for an animal who cannot contribute," he had said.

Jello had been so cowed he was useless. And now he was dead.

Slowly she opened her pack. The food was gone but her needles, ulo, and boots were tucked in the pockets where she had put them. They were now more wonderful to Miyax than airplanes, ocean liners, and great wide bridges. As she put on her shoes she checked for her man's knife and matches. They were there, too. Life was hers again! Slinging her pack to her shoulders, she placed a stone at Jello's head and turned away.

"You've got to be a super-wolf to live," she said. "Poor Jello was not." She left him to the jaegers and foxes.

"Amaroq, wolf, my friend," she sang as she walked along. "Amaroq, my adopted father."

Reaching Point Hope seemed less important, now that she had come to truly understand the value of her ulo and needles. If she missed the boat she could live well until another year. Her voice rang out happily as she sang and followed the birds and her compass.

ONE EVENING AS SHE LOOKED for a campsite, she felt lonely. To amuse herself she thought of the hill where the white house stood in San Francisco. When it seemed almost real enough to touch, and very beautiful, it vanished abruptly; for the tundra was even more beautiful—a glistening gold, and its shadows were purple and blue. Lemon-yellow clouds sailed a green sky and every wind-tossed sedge was a silver thread.

"Oh," she whispered in awe, and stopped where she was to view the painted earth. As she dropped her pack it clanged out a frozen note, reminding her again that autumn was over. The season had been brief; the flash of bird wings, the thunder of migrating herds. That was all. Now it was winter, and the top of the soil was solid. No blue sea would be lapping the shores of Barrow; instead the Arctic Ocean would be a roaring white cauldron forming ice that would join the land with the polar cap.

She was not afraid. Singing her Amaroq song, she gathered grass and rolled it into cylinders. With deft strokes she chopped a hole in the icebound lake, soaked the grass sticks, and laid them out in the air to freeze. Hours later they had snapped and cracked into ice poles. She cut the drag in two pieces and, pushing the poles under one piece, she erected a tent.

Inside her shelter she cut a long thread of hide and twisted it into a snare. A snowshoe rabbit trail ran along the lake and she set off to find the resting place of the one who had made it. The air was cold and she blew her breath into the wolverine trim of her parka hood. There it hung and warmed her face.

Amaroq called and she called back, not to tell him she needed food as she had once done, but to tell him where she was.

A lemming burst out of the grass near her foot and she spun around to look for its nest and young. Not finding them, she turned back in time to see a fox ripple like a ribbon as he pounced and sped off with the lemming. She grinned, made a mental note to be quicker, and walked carefully along the rabbit trail. Finally she came upon a concave dish in the ground—the roost. In it the rabbit would hide from enemies or rest when not eating. She spread her snare, elevated it with an ice stick, and paid out enough hideline to be out of the sight of the hare.

Flat on her stomach she watched the roost. Minutes turned into hours and the pinks and greens of sunset colored the frozen prairie. Suddenly down the trail, ears back, feet flying, came the rabbit. It made a sharp turn and plopped to a halt in its roost. Miyax yanked and caught its left foot. She killed it quickly, and ran back to camp.

The grass rustled and she turned around. "Kapu!"

He was trotting down the rabbit trail with a leg of caribou in his mouth. His head bucked as he fought the awkward weight of the meat.

"Kapu!" she repeated. He wagged his tail, took a better grip on his burden, and trotted up to her. He dropped it at her feet. With a skip and a leap she told in wolf language how glad she was to see him. He replied by dashing around in a small circle, then in three big circles. Finally he stopped and wagged his tail.

"Is this for me?" she asked pointing to the leg. He spanked the ground with his front paw, leaped to the side, and spanked the ground again. With a grin she reached in her pocket, found a strip of caribou hide, and thrust it at him. Kapu snatched it, and with one pull not only wrested it from her, but sent her sprawling on her back. Tail held straight out, he streaked like a rocket across the lichens, turned, and came back with the hide. He shook it in front of her, daring her to take it away.

"You're much too strong for me now, Kapu," she said and slowly got to her feet. "I can't play with you anymore." Shaking the hide, he danced, barked, and then ran over the tundra until he was but a speck in the distance.

Miyax laughed, and dragged the caribou leg back to her tent. She cut it up and built a small fire. She skinned the rabbit, saving the fur to line her new mitten.

As the stew cooked, the crackling cold inspired her to dance. She stepped forward on the vast stage at the top of the world and bowed to her immense audience.

Curving her arms out, bending her knees, she hopped on one foot and beat time with the other. Then she glided and shifted her weight, gracefully executing a combination of steps which the bent woman had danced long ago at seal camp. When she came to the refrain, however, she did not do the dance about evil spirits, but improvised—as Eskimos do at this point. She told the story of a young wolf who had brought the lost girl a shank of meat, and ended the performance with a Kapu-like caper. She spun laughing to a stop. She was warm. Her blood tingled.

"Ee-lie," she thought. "The old Eskimo customs are not so foolish— they have purpose. I'm as warm as the center of a lemming's nest."

As the sky darkened, Kapu came back. He barked softly.

"I know what you want," she called, holding out a large piece of cooked meat. Kapu took it so gently from her fingers that she could not even feel his teeth. As she watched him run off into the night, her eyes lifted to the sky. There, twinkling in the distance, was the North Star, the permanent light that had guided the Eskimos for thousands of years. She sang:

*Bright star, still star*
*Lead me to the sea . . .*

Hastily, she cut the remaining half of her caribou skin into four strips and a circle. Cracking open the ice on the lake, she weighted the pieces with stones and sent them to the bottom.

Around midnight she awoke to hear her wolves in the distance talking softly among themselves—probably paying tribute to Amaroq as they moved along the trail, she thought. Peering out of her tent she saw that the star was gone. A cold flake struck her nose, melted, fell into her fur, and froze. The wind blared, the wolves called joyously, and Miyax snuggled deep in her furs. Let it snow. Kapu had known it was coming and had brought food for her.

She slept until daybreak, saw that it was still snowing, and dozed, off and on, through the white, wild day as the weasels and foxes did. That night the sky cleared, and at dawn she crawled out of her skins. The tundra was white with the snow that would lock up the Arctic till June. The cold had deepened.

After breakfast she cracked open the lake ice again, pulled out the water-soaked circle and laid it out on the ground. Using her man's knife, she turned up the edges, tied them in place, and let the cup freeze in the air. As it hardened she stepped into the bottom, tramped it into a bowl, and then cut two holes in one side. Through these she ran leather thongs and tied them together.

Next she took two strips of skin from the water and held them in place while they froze to the bottom of the bowl, in the shape of flat rockers. Then she stood up. Her sled was done.

Working quickly, for she had only a few hours of daylight, she formed tear-shaped hoops out of the last two strips. These she laid out to freeze. When they were solid she webbed them with hide, made loops for her toes, and put on her snowshoes. They crackled and snapped, but kept her up on the drifts. Now she could travel the top of the snow.

She cut the rest of the caribou leg into bite-size chunks and stored them in her sled. Then, adjusting her mittens in the darkness, she took a bearing on the North Star and started off.

Her icy sled jingled over the wind-swept lakes and she sang as she traveled. The stars grew brighter as the hours passed and the tundra began to glow, for the snow reflected each twinkle a billion times over, turning the night to silver. By this light she could see the footsteps of the wolves. She followed them, for they were going her way.

Just before sunrise the wolf prints grew closer together. They were slowing down for the sleep. She felt their presence everywhere, but could not see them. Running out on a lake, she called. Shadows flickered on the top of a frost heave. There they were! She quickened her stride. She would camp with them and do the dance of the wolf-pup-feeding-the-lost-girl for Kapu. He would surely run in circles when he saw it.

The shadows flattened as she walked, and by the time she reached the other shore they had turned into sky and vanished. There were no footsteps in the snow to say her pack had been there and she knew the Arctic dawn had tricked her eyes. "Frost spirits," she said, as she pitched her tent by the lake and crawled into bed.

By the yellow-green light of the low noon sun Miyax could see that she had camped on the edge of the wintering grounds of the caribou. Their many gleaming antlers formed a forest on the horizon. Such a herd would certainly attract her pack. She crawled out of bed and saw that she had pitched her tent in a tiny forest about three inches high. Her heart pounded excitedly, for she had not seen one of these willow groves since Nunivak. She was making progress, for they grew, not near Barrow, but in slightly warmer and wetter lands near the coast. She smelled the air in the hopes that it bore the salty odor of the ocean, but it smelled only of the cold.

The dawn cracked and hummed and the snow was so fine that it floated above ground when a breeze stirred. Not a bird passed overhead. The buntings, longspurs, and terns were gone from the top of the world.

A willow ptarmigan, the chicken of the tundra, clucked behind her and whistled softly as it hunted seeds. The Arctic Circle had been returned to its permanent bird resident, the hardy ptarmigan. The millions of voices of summer had died down to one plaintive note.

*Aha, ahahahahahaha!* Miyax sat up, wondering what that was. Creeping halfway out of her bag, she peered into the sky to see a great brown bird maneuver its wings and speed west.

"A skua!" She was closer to the ocean than she thought, for the skua is a bird of the coastal waters of the Arctic. As her eyes followed it, they came to rest on an oil drum, the signpost of American civilization in the North. How excited she would have been to see this a month ago; now she was not so sure. She had her ulo and needles, her sled and her tent, and the world of her ancestors. And she liked the simplicity of that world. It was easy to understand. Out here she understood how she fitted into the scheme of the moon and stars and the constant rise and fall of life on the earth. Even the snow was part of her, she melted it and drank it.

Amaroq barked. He sounded as if he was no more than a quarter of a mile away.

"Ow, ooo," she called. Nails answered, and then the whole pack howled briefly.

"I'm over here!" she shouted joyously, jumping up and down. "Here by the lake." She paused. "You know that. You know everything about me all the time."

The wind began to rise as the sun started back to the horizon. The lake responded with a boom that sounded like a pistol shot. The freeze was deepening. Miyax lit a fire and put on her pot. A warm stew would taste good and the smoke and flames would make the tundra home.

Presently Amaroq barked forcefully, and the pack answered. Then the royal voice sounded from another position, and Silver checked in from across the lake. Nails gave a warning snarl and the pups whispered in "woofs." Miyax shaded her eyes; her wolves were barking from points around a huge circle and she was in the middle. This was strange—they almost always stayed together. Suddenly Amaroq barked ferociously, his voice angry and authoritative. Silver yelped, then Nails and Kapu. They had something at bay.

She stepped onto the lake and skipped toward them. Halfway across she saw a dark head rise above the hill, and a beast with a head as large as the moon rose to its hind feet, massive paws swinging.

"Grizzly!" she gasped and stopped stone-still, as the huge animal rushed out onto the ice. Amaroq and Nails leapt at its face and sprang away before the bear could strike. They were heading it off, trying to prevent it from crossing. The bear snarled, lunged forward, and galloped toward Miyax.

She ran toward her tent. The wind was in her face and she realized she was upwind of the bear, her scent blowing right to him. She darted off in another direction, for bears have poor eyesight and cannot track if they cannot smell. Slipping and sliding, she reached the south bank as the grizzly staggered forward, then crumpled to its knees and sat down. She wondered why he was not in hibernation. The wolves had been sleeping all day—they could not have wakened the bear. She sniffed the air to try to smell the cause, but only odorless ice crystals stung her nose.

The pack kept harassing the sleepy beast, barking and snarling, but with no intention of killing it. They were simply trying to drive it away—away from her, she realized.

Slowly the bear got to its feet and permitted itself to be herded up the lake bank and back to where it had come from. Reluctantly, blindly, it staggered before the wolves. Occasionally it stood up like a giant, but mostly it roared in the agony of sleepiness.

Yapping, barking, darting, the wolves drove the grizzly far out on the tundra. Finally they veered away and, breaking into a joyous gallop, dashed over the snow and out of sight. Their duty done, they were running—not to hunt, not to kill—but simply for fun.

Miyax was trembling. She had not realized the size and ferocity of the dark bear of the North, who is called "grizzly" inland, and "brown bear" along the coast—*Ursus arctos*. Large ones, like the grizzly her wolves had driven away, weighed over a thousand pounds and stood nine feet tall when they reared. Miyax wiped a bead of perspiration from her forehead. Had he come upon her tent, with one curious sweep of his paw he would have snuffed out her life while she slept.

"Amaroq, Nails, Kapu," she called. "I thank you. I thank you."

As she packed to travel on, she thought about her escorts. Wolves did not like civilization. Where they had once dwelled all over North America they now lived in remote parts of Canada, in only two of the lower forty-eight states, and in the wilderness of Alaska. Even the roadless North Slope had fewer wolves than it did before the gussaks erected their military bases and brought airplanes, snowmobiles, electricity, and jeeps to the Arctic.

As she thought about the gussaks she suddenly knew why the brown bear was awake. The Americans' hunting season had begun! Her wolves were in danger! The gussaks were paid to shoot them. A man who brought in the left ear of a wolf to the warden was rewarded with a bounty of fifty dollars. The bounty was evil to the old men at seal camp, for it encouraged killing for money, rather than need.

Kapugen considered the bounty the gussaks' way of deciding

that amaroqs could not live on this earth anymore. "And no men have that right," he would say. "When the wolves are gone there will be too many caribou grazing the grass and the lemmings will starve. Without the lemmings the foxes and birds and weasels will die. Their passing will end smaller lives upon which even man depends, whether he knows it or not, and the top of the world will pass into silence."

Miyax was worried. The oil drum she had seen when the skua flew over marked the beginning of civilization and the end of the wilderness. She must warn her pack of the danger ahead. She had learned to say many things to them; but now, the most important of all, the ear-twist or bark that would turn them back, she did not know.

How, she thought, do I shout "Go away! Go far, far away!" She sang:

> Go away, royal wolf,
> Go away, do not follow.
> I'm a gun at your head,
> When I pass the oil drum.

Threads of clouds spun up from the earth and trailed across the tundra. They marked the beginning of a white-out. Miyax changed her plans to travel that night, crept into her shelter, and watched the air turn white as the snow arose from the ground and hung all around her. She closed her tent flap and took out her pot. In it she put a piece of fat from the bladder-bag and a scrap of sinew. She lit the sinew and a flame illuminated her tiny home. She took out the comb.

As she carved she saw that it was not a comb at all, but Amaroq. The teeth were his legs, the handle his head. He was waiting to be released from the bone. Surprised to see him, she carved carefully for hours and finally she let him out. His neck was arched, his head and tail were lifted. Even his ears had a message. "I love you," they said.

A bird called faintly in the darkness. Miyax wondered what kind it was and what it was doing so far north at this date. Too sleepy to think, she unlaced her boots, undressed, and folded her clothes. The bird called from the edge of her sleeping skin. Holding her candle above her head, she crept toward the door and peered into the bright eyes of a golden plover. He was young, for he wore the splotched plumage of the juvenile and still had a trace of baby-yellow around his beak. He slumped against her skins.

Gently she slipped her hand under his feet, picked him up, and brought him close to her. His black and gold feathers gleamed in the sputtering light. She had never beheld a plover so closely and now understood why Kapugen had called them "the spirit of the birds." The plover's golden eye and red noseband made it look like one of the dancers in the Bladder Feast.

"You are lost," she said. "You should be far from here. Perhaps in Labrador. Perhaps even in your winter home on the plains of Argentina. And so you are dying. You need insects and meat. But I'm so glad you're here." Then she added, "I shall call you Tornait, the bird spirit."

She eased the bird inside her warm sleeping skin, cut off a small piece of caribou meat, and held it out. Tornait ate ravenously, then rested. She fed him once more, and then he tucked his head in his back feathers and went to sleep.

The following night the white-out was still so dense she could not see the ground when she crept out for snow to melt and drink.

"I won't go on tonight," she said to Tornait when she came inside. "But I do not care. I have food, light, furs, fire, and a pretty companion." That evening she polished her carving of Amaroq and talked to Tornait. The plover was incredibly tame, perhaps because he lived in the most barren parts of the world where there were no people, perhaps because he was lonely. Tornait ran over her skins, flitted to her head and shoulders, and sang when she sang.

On the next afternoon the white-out was but a frosty mist. Miyax was cooking dinner when Tornait drew his feathers to his body and stood up in alarm. She listened for a long time before she heard the snow scream as footsteps pressed it. Scrambling to the door, she saw Kapu in the mist, frost on his whiskers.

"Hi!" she called. He did not turn around for he was looking at something in the distance. Presently Amaroq swept into view and stopped beside him.

"Amaroq!" she shouted. "Amaroq, how are you?" Tossing her head in wolf happiness, she crawled out of her tent on all fours and nudged him under the chin. He arched his neck grandly. Then, with a glance at Kapu, he ran out on the lake. The young wolf followed, and, laughing joyously, Miyax crawled after them both. She had not gone far before Amaroq stopped and glared at her. She stayed where she was. The regal pair leaped away, snow billowing up from their strides like smoke.

Getting to her knees she looked for Silver, Nails, and the other pups, but they did not follow the pair. Miyax rocked back on her heels. Could it be that the leader of the pack was teaching the leader of the pups? She nodded slowly as she comprehended. Of course. To be a leader required not only fearlessness and intelligence, but experience and schooling. The head of a wolf pack needed to be trained, and who better to do this than Amaroq?

"And I know what you'll teach," she called out. "You'll teach him which animal to harvest. You'll teach him to make all decisions. You'll teach him how to close in on a caribou, and where to bed the wolf pack down; and you'll teach him to love and protect."

The white-out vanished, the stars blazed out, and San Francisco called to Miyax. It was time to move on. Kapu was now in school.

"But how shall I tell them not to follow me anymore?" she asked Tornait as she crawled back into her tent.

"Of course!" she gasped. She had been told by Amaroq himself how to say "stay back" when he had wanted Kapu alone. He had walked forward, turned around, and glared into her eyes. She had stopped in her tracks and gone home. Eagerly she practiced. She ran forward, looked over her shoulder, and glared.

"Stay Amaroq. Stay where you are!"

Humming to herself she took down her tent, rolled it into a bundle, and threw it on the new sled. Then she stuffed her pack and tucked Tornait in the hood of her parka. Sticking her toes in her new snowshoes, she took a bearing on the constant star. The snow squeaked under her feet, and for the first time she felt the dry bite of the cold right through her parka and boots. To her this meant the temperature was zero, the point every year when she began to feel chilly. Dancing and swinging her arms to get warm, she picked up the thongs of her sled and walked toward the sea. The sled glided lightly behind her.

She did not hear the airplane; she saw it. The low sun of noon struck its aluminum body and it sparkled like a star in the sky. It was a small plane, the type bush pilots use to carry people over the roadless tundra and across the rugged mountains of Alaska where cars cannot go. Presently its sound reached her ears and the throb of the engines reminded her that this was the beginning of the season when bush pilots took the gussaks out to hunt. The craft tipped its wings and zigzagged across the sky. When it continued to zag she realized the pilot was following a meandering river where game wintered. A river, she thought; rivers led to the sea. I am nearing the end of my journey; Point Hope might be but one sleep away. She quickened her pace.

The airplane banked, turned, and came toward her. It seemed as big as an eagle as it skimmed low over the ground. Bright flashes of fire burst from its side.

"They *are* hunting," she said to Tornait. "Let's get in the oil drum. I look like a bear in these clothes."

Just before she reached the drum she crossed the steps of Amaroq and Kapu. They had passed this way only moments ago, for the snow crystals their warm feet had melted were not yet frozen again. The plane continued to come toward her. Apparently she had been seen. She kicked snow over her sled and pack and crawled to the front of the barrel. It was sealed. She could not get inside. Scurrying to the other end she found that it, too, was closed. Desperately she threw herself under the curve of the drum and lay still. Much of her was still exposed. Flailing her hands and feet, she stirred up the light snow. It arose like a cloud and settled upon her as the plane soared above.

Shots rang out. The plane roared away and Miyax opened her eyes. She was still alive and the air hunters were over the river. The plane banked and flew back, this time very low. Tornait struggled.

"Be still," she said. The gunfire snapped again and, eyes wide open, she saw that it was not aimed at her.

"Amaroq!" Horrified, she watched him leap into the air as a splatter of shots burst beside him. Digging in his claws, he veered to the right and left as Kapu ran to join him. Teeth bared, angrily growling, Amaroq told him to go. Kapu sped off. The plane hesitated, then pursued Amaroq.

Shots hit the snow in front of him. He reared and turned.

"Amaroq!" she screamed. "Here! Come here!"

The plane swerved, dove, and skimmed about thirty feet above the ground. Its guns blasted. Amaroq stumbled, pressed back his ears, and galloped across the tundra like a shooting star. Then he reared, and dropped in the snow.

He was dead.

"For a bounty," she screamed. "For money, the magnificent Amaroq is dead!" Her throat constricted with grief, and sobs choked her.

The plane banked and came back. Kapu was running to Amaroq. His ears were pressed to his head and his legs moved so swiftly they were a blur. Bullets showered the snow around him. He leaped, dodged, and headed for the oil drum. His wide eyes and open mouth told Miyax he was afraid for the first time in his life. Blindly he ran, and as he came by she reached out and tripped him. He sprawled across the snow and lay still. While the plane coasted off to make another turn, she covered Kapu with flakes.

The snow turned red with blood from his shoulder. Miyax rolled under the barrel.

The air exploded and she stared up into the belly of the plane. Bolts, doors, wheels, red, white, silver, and black, the plane flashed before her eyes. In that instant she saw great cities, bridges, radios, school books. She saw the pink room, long highways, TV sets, telephones, and electric lights. Black exhaust enveloped her, and civilization became this monster that snarled across the sky.

The plane shrank before her eyes, then turned and grew big again. Tornait flew to the top of the barrel, screaming his alarm cry and beating his wings.

Kapu tried to get up.

"Don't move," Miyax whispered. "They're coming for Amaroq." Knowing Kapu did not understand, she reached out and softly stroked him, singing: "Lie still. Lie still." She watched him slump back in the snow without a sound.

The plane returned at so low a level she could see the men in the cockpit, their coat collars pulled up around their necks, their crash helmets and goggles gleaming. They were laughing and watching the ground. Desperately Miyax thought about Silver, Nails, and the pups. Where were they? They must be clear targets on the white snow. Maybe not—they were light in color, not black.

Suddenly the engine accelerated, the wing flaps pressed down, and the craft climbed, banked, and sailed down the river like a migrating bird. It did not turn around.

Miyax buried her fingers in Kapu's fur. "They did not even stop to get him!" she cried. "They did not even kill him for money. I don't understand. I don't understand. *Ta vun ga vun ga,*" she cried. "*Pisupa gasu punga.*" She spoke of her sadness in Eskimo, for she could not recall any English.

Kapu's blood spread like fish ripples on the snow. She wriggled to him and clamped her thumb on the vein that was gushing. She held the pressure—a minute, an hour—she did not know how long. Then Tornait called hungrily. Cautiously she lifted her hand. The bleeding had stopped.

"*Ta gasu*," she said to Kapu. She brushed the snow off her sled and took out her poles. She set up her tent beside the barrel, banked the snow around the bottom to seal out the wind, and spread her ground cloth under it. When she tried to push Kapu into the shelter she found him too heavy. He lifted his head, then dropped it wearily. Miyax decided to build the tent around him. She took everything down and started all over again.

This time she eased the ground skin under him inch by inch until he lay on the fur. Then she kicked the oil drum to free it from the ice, rolled it close to him, and erected her tent against it. She sealed the gaps with snow.

The drum was old, for it had different markings than those around Barrow, but like them, it was barely rusted. The frigid winters and the dry desert-like conditions of the tundra prevent metals, papers, garbage, and refuse from deteriorating as it does in warmer zones. In the Arctic, all artifacts are preserved for ages. Even throwing them into the oceans does not work a change, for the water freezes around them, and in the ice floes they come back on the shores. The summer sun unveils them again.

Miyax melted snow, cut off meat for Tornait, and fed him. He flew down from the barrel and ran into the tent. Hopping onto her furry sleeping skin, he puffed his feathers, stood on one foot, and went to sleep.

With the stew bubbling, Kapu resting, and Tornait asleep, Miyax dared to think of Amaroq. She would go and bid him good-bye. She tried to get up, but she could not move. Grief held her in a vise-like clamp.

About an hour later Kapu lifted his head, rolled his eyes around the cozy interior of the tent, and accepted chunks of stew. Miyax petted his head and told him in Eskimo to lie still while she looked at his wound. It was long and deep and she knew it must be sewn together.

Taking a piece of sinew from the ground skin, she threaded it into her needle and pierced the soft flesh. Kapu growled.

"*Xo lur pajau, sexo,*" she sang soothingly. "*Lupir pajau se suri vanga pangmane majo riva pangmane.*" Monotonously repeating over and over the healing song of the old bent lady, she hypnotized Kapu as she closed the wound. The perspiration was running down her cheeks when she was done, but she was able to tell him that he would get well and return to lead their pack.

The sun set in a navy blue sky, and the stars sparkled on and off as they spoke of their vast distances from the earth. About midnight the inside of the tent began to glow green and Kapu's eyes shone like emeralds. Miyax peered out the flap door. Fountains of green fire rose from the earth and shot to the top of the black velvet sky. Red and white lights sprayed out of the green. The northern lights were dancing. The lakes boomed, and Nails howled mournfully beyond the tent.

Miyax howled back to tell him where she was. Then Silver barked and the pups called, too. Each voice sounded closer than the last; the pack was coming toward the oil drum as they searched for Amaroq and Kapu.

Miyax stepped into the light of the aurora. It was time to bid Amaroq farewell. She tried to go forward but her feet would not move. Grief still held them useless. Clutching her left knee in both hands, she lifted her foot and put it down; then she lifted the other and put it down, slowly making her way across the turquoise snow.

Amaroq lay where he had fallen, his fur shining in the strange magnetic light.

"Amaroq . . ." She took her carving from her pocket, and got down on her knees. Singing softly in Eskimo, she told him she had no bladder for his spirit to dwell in, but that she had his totem. She asked him to enter the totem and be with her forever.

For a long time she held the carving over his body. Presently, the pain in her breast grew lighter and she knew the wolf was with her.

The stars had slipped down the sky when at last she stood up and walked swiftly back to Kapu.

All night Miyax sat beside him and listened to Silver, Nails, and the pups.

"*Ow ow ow ow owwwwwww,*" they cried in a tone she had never heard before, and she knew they were crying for Amaroq.

THE SUN WENT DOWN on November tenth not to rise again for sixty-six days. In the darkness Kapu got up to exercise by walking out on the tundra and back. Tornait was not so comfortable in the continuous night. He slept in Miyax's furs most of the time, waiting for the dawn. When it did not come, hunger awoke him; he ran from his roost to Miyax, pecked on her boot, and fluttered his wings for food. Then the darkness would say to him "sleep," and he would run back to his roost, pull his foot into his breast feathers, and close his eyes.

For her part, Miyax found the clear nights quite manageable. She could hunt caribou chips by star and moonlight, cook outside, and even sew. When the sky was overcast, however, the tundra was black and she would stay inside, light her candle, and talk to Kapu and Tornait.

At these times she began to shape the antler-weapon into a more elaborate design. As she worked she saw five puppies in it. Carefully she carved out their ears and toes until they were running in single file, Kapu in the lead. She grew tired, took out Amaroq's totem, and thought about his life and brave spirit.

"The pink room is red with your blood," she said. "I cannot go there. But where can I go? Not back to Barrow and Daniel. Not back to Nunivak and Martha . . . and you cannot take care of me anymore."

Snowstorms came and went; the wind blew constantly. One starry night Miyax heard a whimper and opened the tent flap to see Silver at the door. She had a large hare in her mouth, and although Miyax was glad for food, she was distressed to realize that her pack was not eating well. Disorganized without Amaroq, they were forced to hunt rabbits and small game. These would not sustain them. Miyax reached out, petted Silver on the shoulder, and felt her bony back. Without a leader the pack would not live through the winter.

Silver nudged her hand, Miyax opened the flap wider, and the beautiful wolf came in. She dropped the rabbit and walked over to Kapu. He got to his feet, and arching his neck, lifted his head above hers. She greeted him, wagging her tail excitedly. Then she tried to bite the top of his nose to tell him she was the leader, but Kapu drew up tall. Gently he took her nose in his mouth. She bit him under the chin, hailing the new chief.

Kapu pushed past her and slipped out of the tent. Silver followed the prince of the wolves.

In the darkness he sang of his leadership, but, too weak to run, turned wearily back to the tent.

A new grandeur attended his movements as he came through the door and Miyax squeezed his chin. He lay down and watched her skin the rabbit.

She gave him the flesh and went out to hunt lemmings for herself. Since the end of summer the little rodents had doubled, tripled, even quadrupled their numbers. By following their runways she found seven nests and caught eighty furred young. She skinned and cooked them, and found them delicious. The next night Silver brought her a part of a moose. She had not killed it, for it was old and frozen. Miyax knew she had been down to the river. No moose wandered the tundra.

Several sleeps later Kapu ran over the snow without stumbling and Miyax decided it was time to move to the river. Game would be more abundant in the dwarf willows that bordered the waterways. There rabbits and ptarmigan gathered to eat seeds out of the wind, and moose wintered on the twigs of the willows. Perhaps Silver and Nails would find a sick yearling and with help from the pups be able to kill it. Life would be kinder there.

She packed, put Tornait in her parka hood and, picking up her sled ropes, set off once more. Kapu limped as he walked beside her, but less and less as he plodded along. The exercise seemed to help him and by the end of the night he was running fifty steps to her one. Often he took her hand and mouthed it affectionately.

The river would not be hard to find, for she had marked its position by the faithful North Star and so, hours later, as the constellation of the hunter moved to the other side of her, she reached the brushy bank. In the distance loomed the massive wall of the Brooks Range, the massive mountains that rimmed the North Slope on the south. Her journey was coming to an end. The rivers that flow out of the Brooks Range are close to the sea.

After making camp Miyax and Kapu went out to snare ptarmigan and rabbits. Silver called from a short distance away and they answered her.

Hours later when Miyax crawled into her sleeping skin the wolves were so near that she could hear the pups scratching the snow as they made their beds.

As she had anticipated, the hunting was excellent, and upon

checking her snares the next day she found three rabbits and two ptarmigan. For several days she was busy skinning and cooking.

One night while Miyax sewed a new boot, Kapu licked her ear and trotted off. When he did not come back by the time the moon had swung all the way around her tent and was back again, a whole day, she went out to look for him. The snow glowed blue and green and the constellations glittered, not only in the sky, but on the ice in the river and on the snow on the bushes and trees. There was, however, no sign of Kapu. She was about to go to bed when the horizon quivered and she saw her pack running the bank. Kapu was in the lead. She crawled into her tent and awakened Tornait.

"Kapu's leading the hunt. All's well," she said. "And now we must leave them."

At dawn she hastily took down her tent, hoisted her pack to her back, and stepped onto the frozen river where walking was easier. Many miles along her way she came upon wolverine tracks and followed them up to a den. There, as she suspected, lay several rabbits and ptarmigan. She loaded them on her sled and returned to the river, listening to Tornait peep soft plover songs in the warmth of her parka hood.

She kissed his beak gently. They were helping each other. She kept him warm and fed him and he radiated heat in her hood. But more important, his whisperings kept her from being totally and hopelessly lonely without Kapu and her wolf pack.

With every mile she traveled now, the oil drums became more and more numerous and the tracks of the wolverine more and more scarce. Like the wolf, the wolverine is an animal of the wilderness, and when Miyax saw no more tracks she knew she was approaching man. One night she counted fifty drums on a spit in the river, and there she made camp. She must stop and think about what she wanted to do.

When she thought of San Francisco, she thought about the airplane and the fire and blood and the flashes and death. When she took out her needle and sewed, she thought about peace and Amaroq.

She knew what she had to do. Live like an Eskimo—hunt and carve and be with Tornait.

The next day she took out her man's knife and cut blocks of snow. These she stacked and shaped into a house that was generously large. If she was going to live as the Eskimos once lived, she needed a home, not just a camp.

When her ice house was completed and her skins were spread over the floor, she sat down and took out the totem of Amaroq. Her fingers had rubbed him to a soft glow in her pocket and he looked rich and regal. Placing him over her door, she blew him a kiss, and as she did so, happiness welled up in her. She knew he was taking care of her spirit.

Time passed, fountains of the magnetic northern lights came and went, and the moon waxed and waned many times. Miyax found her life very satisfying. She became an expert at catching small game and she took great pleasure in carving. When she had finished the carving of the puppies, she found a stone by the river and began chipping it into an owl. Always she listened for her pack, but they did not call. She was both glad and miserable.

Miyax was not without things to do. When she was not hunting, or carving, she danced, sewed, chopped wood or made candles. Sometimes she tried to spell Eskimo words with the English alphabet. Such beautiful words must be preserved forever.

One night she began a tiny coat of ptarmigan feathers for Tornait. He had been shivering lately, even in her parka hood, and she was concerned about him. She stitched the plumes to a paper-thin rabbit hide and fashioned a bird-like coat.

On the moonrise when the coat was finished and she was trying to slip it on Tornait, she heard in the distance the crackle of feet on the ice. The sound grew louder and she poked her head into the night to see a man on the river running beside his sled and team of dogs. Her heart leaped—an Eskimo hunter, one of her own pack, truly. Rushing onto the river ice she waited until the sled drew close.

"Ayi!" she called.

"Ayi!" a voice answered, and within minutes the hunter pulled the sled up beside her and greeted her warmly. Nestled in the furs was the man's woman and child. Their eyes glistened softly in the moonlight.

Miyax's voice was hoarse from disuse, but she managed to greet them happily in Eskimo and invite them into her house for a sleep. The woman was glad to stop, she told Miyax in Yupik dialect, as she climbed from the sled. They had not rested since they had left Kangik, a town on Kuk Bay at the mouth of the Avalik River, the river they were on.

At last Miyax knew where she was. Kangik was inland from Wainwright and still many sleeps from Point Barrow. But she no longer cared.

"I'm Roland," the man said in English as he unloaded his sleeping skins on the floor of the igloo and spread them out. "Are you alone?"

Miyax smiled at him as if she did not understand and put a twisted spruce log on the fire. When it blazed and man and woman were warming their backs, Roland asked her again, but this time in Yupik, her own beautiful tongue. She answered that she was.

"I'm Alice," the pretty mother said. Miyax gestured hopelessly. "Uma," the woman said, pointing to herself. "Atik," she said, pointing to the man and, lifting the baby above her head, called him Sorqaq. Miyax found the names so nice that, as she took her cooking pot from the fire to offer her guests hot ptarmigan, she hummed and sang. Then she went to her sleeping skin, picked up Tornait, and held him before Sorqaq, who was now on his mother's back in her kuspuck. He peeked over her shoulder, laughed at the bird, kicked, and disappeared. In his excitement he had lost his knee grip and dropped to his mother's belt. Miyax laughed aloud. Uma giggled and gave him a boost; his round face reappeared and he reached for the bird.

Miyax suddenly wanted to talk. Speaking rapidly in Yupik, she told her guests about the river, the game, the fuel, and the stars—but not about the wolves or her past. They listened and smiled.

When dinner was over Atik talked slowly and softly, and Miyax learned that Kangik was an Eskimo village with an airport and a mission school. A generator had been built, and electricity lighted the houses in winter. A few men even owned snowmobiles there. Atik was proud of his town.

Before going to bed he went out to feed the dogs. Then Uma talked. She said they were headed for the mountains to hunt caribou. When Atik returned, Miyax told him he did not need to go to the mountains—that a large herd was yarded not far up the river. She drew a map on the floor and showed him where the wintering grounds of the caribou lay. He was happy to learn this, he said, for the Brooks Range was treacherous in winter; whole mountainsides avalanched, and storms brewed up in mere minutes.

Uma nursed the baby, tucked him into their furs, and softly sang him to sleep as the fire began to die down. Presently her head nodded, and she slipped into bed, where Atik joined her.

Miyax alone was awake, visions of Kangik filling her head. She would go there and be useful. Perhaps she would teach children how to snare rabbits, make parkas, and carve; or she might live with some family that needed her help. She might even work in the store. In Kangik she would live as her ancestors had, in rhythm with the animals and the climate. She would stay far away from San Francisco where men were taught to kill without reason. She did not fall asleep for hours.

Tornait awoke first and called softly. Miyax dressed, cut off a piece of meat, and held it out to him. He snatched the food and swallowed it noisily. That awoke the baby and the baby awoke Uma, who reached out, took him to her breast, and rocked him as she lay in the furry warmth of her skins. It was almost zero in the house and she did not hurry to get up.

Atik awoke, yawned, and roared, "I'm hungry." Uma laughed and Miyax put the pot on the fire. Atik dressed, went out to his sled, and brought back bacon, bread, beans, and butter. Miyax had forgotten there were such good things and her mouth fairly watered as she smelled them cooking. At first she refused the food when Uma offered it, but seeing how disappointed she was she accepted the bacon and sucked on it quietly, remembering with pain the tastes of Barrow.

After breakfast Atik went out to harness the dogs, Miyax cleaned up, and Uma played with her baby. As she tossed him she chatted happily about her love for Atik and how excited she had been when he decided to take her on the hunt. Most Eskimo wives were left home these days; with the advent of gussak frozen foods, cooks were no longer needed for the hunt. And the women never tanned hides anymore; all skins for the tourist trade must go to Seattle to be tanned correctly for the temperate climates where most were shipped.

Uma rambled on. Atik had been raised in Anchorage and knew very little about hunting, for his father had been a mechanic. But he had died, and Atik was sent to live with his grandfather in Kangik. He had become enamored of hunting and fishing and became so skilled that when his grandfather died he was adopted by the greatest of all living Eskimo hunters.

"Kapugen taught Atik where the seals live and how to smell a caribou trail."

Miyax stopped cleaning her pot. Her blood raced hot, then cold. Turning slowly around she stared at Uma.

"Where was this Kapugen born?" she asked in Eskimo.

"He has never said. He paddled up the river one day, beached his kayak, and built a house where he landed. All I know is that he came out of the Bering Sea. But he was wealthy in the Eskimo sense—intelligent, fearless, full of love—and he soon became a leader of Kangik."

Miyax did not take her eyes off Uma's lips as they formed soft words of Kapugen. *"U i ya Kangik?"* she asked.

"Yes, but not in the center of town where the rich men live. Although Kapugen is also rich, he lives in a simple green house on the river bank. It is upstream, beside the wilderness, where the people he loves feel free to visit."

Trembling with eagerness, Miyax asked Uma to tell her more about Kapugen, and Uma, spilling over with enthusiasm, told how the town and its people had grown poor and hungry several years ago. The walrus had all but vanished from the coast; the gray whales were rare, and the seals were few and far between. The Bureau of Indian Affairs put most everyone on pensions, and so they drank and forgot all they knew. Then Kapugen arrived. He was full of pride and held his head high. He went out into the wilderness and came back with musk-oxen. These he bred and raised. The men helped him; the women made the fur into thread and then into mittens and beautiful sweaters and scarves. These were sold to the gussaks who paid high prices for them, and within a few years the people of Kangik became independent and prosperous.

"But there is still a need for caribou and wolverine furs for clothing and trim," she said, "so Kapugen and Atik go hunting every winter to supply the town."

"Kapugen did not come this year," she went on. "He let me come instead." She smiled, slipped her baby into her kuspuck, tightened her belt, and stood up. "Kapugen is wise and strong."

Miyax turned her back to Uma. She must not see the quivering of her body at every mention of her father's name. He had been dead to her, for so long that she was almost frightened by the knowledge that he lived. Yet she loved each cold chill that told her it was true.

Outside the dogs began fighting over their rations, and Atik's whip cracked like a gunshot. Miyax shivered at the sound. She thought of Amaroq and tears welled in her eyes but did not fall, for she was also thinking about Kapugen. She must find him. He would save the wolves just as he had saved the people of Kangik.

"Amaroq, Amaroq," she sang as she fluffed up her furs. Uma turned to her in surprise.

"You are happy after all," she said in Eskimo. "I thought perhaps this was the beginning of your periods and that your family had sent you to a hut to be alone. The old grandmother who raised me did that, and I was miserable and so unhappy, because no one does that anymore."

Miyax shook her head. "I am not yet a woman."

Uma did not inquire further, but hugged her. Then she put her baby in her kuspuck and crept out the door to join Atik in the starlit darkness. It was day and the constellations of the Southern Hemisphere were shining overhead. The dogs were biting their harnesses and fighting each other, and Atik was trying to make them hold still. Suddenly they lunged in all directions and the sled was moving. Atik picked up Uma and the baby, put them on the sled and, calling his grateful thanks to Miyax, took off.

She waved until they were lost in the darkness, then rushed into her house, rolled up her sleeping skins, and loaded her sled. She hoisted her pack to her back and picked up Tornait. Carefully she slipped the feather coat around his breast and, leaving his wings free, tied the little coat on his back. He looked silly. She laughed, rubbed her nose against his beak, and tucked him into the hood of her parka.

"*Amna a-ya, a-ya-amna,*" she sang as she slid to the river, put on her snowshoes, and strode down the snapping ice bed.

She had gone about a mile when she heard Kapu bark. She knew it was he. His voice was unmistakable. Terrified, she turned around.

"Stay! Stay!" she screamed. The wind picked up her words and blew them down the river. Kapu ran up to her, followed by Nails and the pups. All were yipping authoritatively as they told her to join them.

"I cannot," she cried. "My own Amaroq lives. I must go to him!"

She walked forward a few steps, and turned and glared as the wolf leader had done. For a moment they hesitated, as if not believing her message. Then they dashed away and ran up the river. They called from the bank, and then they were gone.

Miyax had spoken her last words to her wolves.

She thought of Kapugen and hurried on. What would she say to him? Would they rub noses when they met? Surely he would hug his favorite child and let her enter his house, tan his hides, sew his clothes, cook his food. There was so much she could do for this great hunter now; prepare caribou, catch rabbits, pluck birds, and even make tools with water and the freezing air. She would be very useful to him and they would live as they were meant to live—with the cold and the birds and the beasts.

She tried to recall Kapugen's face—his dark eyes and the brows that drooped kindly. Would his cheeks still be strong and creased by laughter? Would he still have long hair and stand tall? A green fountain of magnetic light shot up into the sky, its edges rimmed with sparks. The air crackled, the river groaned, and Miyax pointed her boots toward Kapugen.

SHE COULD SEE THE VILLAGE of Kangik long before she got to it. Its lights twinkled in the winter night on the first bench of the river near the sea. When she could make out windows and the dark outlines of houses, she pulled her sled to the second bench above the river and stopped. She needed to think before meeting Kapugen.

She pitched her tent and spread out her sleeping skins. Lying on her stomach, she peered down on the town. It consisted of about fifty wooden houses. A few were large, but all had the same rectangular design with peaked roof. Kangik was so snowy she could not see if there was trash in the streets, but even if there had been she would not have cared. Kapugen's home had to be beautiful.

The village had one crossroad, where the church and mission stood. On either side of them were the stores, which Miyax recognized by the many people who wandered in and out. She listened. Dog teams barked from both ends of town, and although she knew there were snowmobiles, the village was essentially a sled-dog town—an old-fashioned Eskimo settlement. That pleased her.

Her eyes roamed the street. A few children were romping in the snow and she guessed that it was about ten o'clock in the morning—the time Eskimo children were sent out to play. By that hour their mothers had completed their morning chores, and had time to dress the little ones and send them outside, cold as it was.

Below the town, she could see the musk-oxen Uma had spoken about. They were circled together near the gate of their enclosure, heads facing out to protect themselves from wolves and bears. Her heart thrilled to see these wondrous oxen of the north. She could help Kapugen take care of the herd.

Two children burst out of a house, put a board across a barrel like a seesaw, and took their positions standing on either end of the board. They began jumping, sending each other higher and higher, and coming down on the board with incredible accuracy. Miyax had seen this game in Barrow, and she watched the flying figures with fascination. Then she slowly lifted her eyes and concentrated on the houses.

There were two green houses near the wilderness. She was debating which one was Kapugen's when the door opened in the smaller one and three children tumbled out. She decided he must live in the other one—with the windows, the annex, and two wooden boats in the yard.

A woman came out of Kapugen's house and hurried across the snow.

"Of course," Miyax thought. "He has married. He has someone to sew and cook for him. But I can still help him with the oxen."

The woman passed the church and stopped at the mission door. She was engulfed in light for an instant, then the door closed behind her. Miyax arose. It was time to seek out her father. He would be alone.

Her feet skimmed the snow as she ran down the hill and across the road, where the children were hitching a dog to a sled. They giggled, and Tornait answered their high bird-like voices from inside her hood.

As Miyax neared the green house she took Tornait in her hand and ran right up to the door. She knocked.

Footsteps sounded from a far corner of the house. The door opened and there stood Kapugen. He was just as she remembered him—rugged, but with dark gentle eyes. Not a word came to her mind. Not even his name or a greeting. She was too moved by the sight of him to speak. Then Tornait peeped. She held him out.

"I have a present for you," she said at last in Eskimo. The feather coat rustled and Tornait's amber head pulled into the covering like a turtle.

"What is it?" Kapugen's voice was resonant and warm and seemed to come from the seashore at Nunivak where the birds sang and the sea was framed with the fur of his parka. "Come in. I've never seen such a bird." He spoke English and she smiled and shook her head. He repeated his invitation in Yupik. Miyax stepped across the threshold and into his home.

The big room was warm and smelled of skins and fat. Harpoons hung on the wall, and under the window was a long couch of furs. The kayak hung from the ceiling, and a little stove glowed in the center of the room. Kapugen's house in Kangik looked just like Kapugen's house in seal camp. She was home.

Tornait hopped to the floor, his feather coat blooming behind him like a courting ptarmigan. He ran under a fur.

"He wears a coat!" Kapugen laughed and got down on his knees to peer at the bird.

"Yes," Miyax said. "He is the spirit of the birds. He is a golden plover."

"A golden plover, the spirit of the birds? Where did you hear that?" Kapugen arose and pushed back her parka hood.

"Who are you?"

"Julie Edwards Miyax Kapugen."

The great frost-blackened hands ran softly over her face.

"Ee-lie," he whispered. "Yes, you are she. You are beautiful like your mother." He opened his arms. She ran into them and for a long time he held her tightly.

"When they sent you to school," he said softly, "Nunivak was too much to bear. I left and began a new life. Last year when at last I was rich I went back to get you. You were gone." His fingers touched her hair and he hugged her once more.

The door opened and the woman came in. "Who have we here?" she asked in English.

Miyax saw her face was pale and her hair was reddish gold. A chill spread over her. What had Kapugen done? What had happened to him that he would marry a gussak? What was his new life?

Kapugen and his woman talked—she loudly, Kapugen quietly. Miyax's eyes went around the room again. This time she saw not just the furs and the kayak, but electric lamps, a radio-phonograph, cotton curtains and, through the door of the annex, the edge of an electric stove, a coffee pot, and china dishes.

There were bookshelves and a framed picture on the wall of some American country garden. Then she saw a helmet and goggles on a chair. Miyax stared at them until Kapugen noticed her.

"Aw, that," he said. "I now own an airplane, Miyax. It's the only way to hunt today. The seals are scarce and the whales are almost gone; but sportsmen can still hunt from planes."

Miyax heard no more. It could not be, it could not be. She would not let it be. She instantly buried what she was thinking in the shadows of her mind.

"Miyax," the wife said in bad Yupik. "I teach in the school here. We shall enroll you tomorrow. You can learn to read and write English. It's very difficult to live even in this Eskimo town without knowing English."

Miyax looked at Kapugen. "I am on my way to San Francisco," she said softly in Yupik. "The gussaks in Wainwright have arranged trans-portation for me. I shall go tomorrow."

A telephone rang. Kapugen answered it and jotted down a note.

"I'll be right back," he said to Miyax. "I'll be right back. Then we'll talk." He hugged her. Miyax stiffened and looked at the helmet.

"Ellen, fix her some food," he called as he put on his coat, a long American-made Arctic field jacket. He zipped it with a flourish and went out the door. Ellen went into the kitchen and Miyax was alone.

Slowly she picked up Tornait, put on her sealskin parka, and placed the little bird in her hood. Then she snapped on the radio, and as it crackled, whined, and picked up music, she opened the door and softly closed it behind her. Kapugen, after all, was dead to her.

On the second bench of the river above town she found her tent and pack, threw them onto her sled and, bending forward, hauled on it. She walked on up the river toward her house. She was an Eskimo, and as an Eskimo she must live. The hour of the lemming was upon the land, cycling slowly toward the hour of Miyax. She would build snow-houses in winter, a sod house in summer. She would carve and sew and trap. And someday there would be a boy like herself. They would raise children, who would live with the rhythm of the beasts and the land.

"The seals are scarce and the whales are almost gone," she heard Kapugen say. "When are you coming to live with us in San Francisco?" called Amy.

Miyax walked backward, watching the river valley. When the last light of Kangik disappeared, the stars lit the snow and the cold deep-ened far below zero. The ice thundered and boomed, roaring like drumbeats across the Arctic.

Tornait peeped. Miyax turned her head, touched him with her chin, and felt his limpness. She stopped walking and lifted him into the cold.

"Tornait. What is wrong with you? Are you sick?" Swiftly opening her pack, she took out some meat, chewed it to thaw it, and gave it to the bird. He refused to eat. She put him inside her parka and pitched her tent out of the wind. When she had banked it with snow, she lit a small fire. The tent glowed, then warmed. Tornait lay in her hands, his head on her fingers; he peeped softly and closed his eyes.

Many hours later she buried him in the snow. The totem of Amaroq was in her pocket. Her fingers ran over it but she did not take it out. She sang to the spirit of Amaroq in her best English.

*The seals are scarce and the whales are almost gone.*
*The spirits of the animals are passing away.*
*Amaroq, Amaroq, you are my adopted father.*
*My feet dance because of you.*
*My eyes see because of you.*
*My mind thinks because of you. And it thinks, on this*
   *thundering night,*
*That the hour of the wolf and the Eskimo is over.*

Julie pointed her boots toward Kapugen.

# Related Readings

# The Wolves

**Alice Cary**

## from *Jean Craighead George*

*This chapter from Alice Cary's biography gives an account of a trip to Alaska Jean Craighead George makes with her son. Although the purpose of the trip was to gather information for a magazine article, some of George's experiences and observations found their way into* Julie of the Wolves.

## Wolves

From the moment she set foot in Barrow, Alaska, Jean felt as though she were in another world. She had taken Professor Carpenter's suggestion seriously about studying wolves—she had traveled to the Arctic Circle to write an article about them for *Reader's Digest*. It was the summer of 1970 and she had brought along 13-year-old Luke. Twig and Craig were busy with summer jobs.

Fog had kept Jean and Luke in Fairbanks for two days, but finally it lifted enough for their plane to land. There were no trees on this northern edge of the state, just the Arctic Ocean, ice, oil barrels, abandoned machinery, and a few buildings and houses.

One of the first things they saw was a small native girl walking in the distance, into nothingness. She was an Inupiat Eskimo—an Eskimo who spoke a dialect[1] called Inupiaq. She looked young to be alone, but she looked determined. *Where is she going?* Jean wondered. *What is her life like?*

Everywhere they looked, things were different. The Top-of-the-World Hotel sounded as though it might be posh, but, with no flush

---

1. **dialect** form of language spoken in a specific region, community, or social group

toilets or running water, it was hardly elegant. The hotel clerk pointed to a cooler and explained that here in Barrow, water came from melting iceberg chips.

After a lunch of reindeer soup, the Georges decided to explore. Along the beach they spotted a sealskin boat beside a huge bowhead whale. The Inupiat Eskimos had made a kill and were carving the meat, using everything possible for one purpose or another. Jean and Luke watched for quite some time. After several hours, the whalers towed the remaining skeleton back to the water, a gift to the sea, in hopes that more whales would come their way.

That evening Jean and Luke ate whale meat. It was tender and delicious, tasting of the ocean. Then came the time Luke had been waiting for—night. He was excited because in Barrow, Alaska, it never gets dark in the summer. (Similarly, because of the way the earth spins around the sun, in winter, it is *always* dark there.) At midnight Jean and Luke returned to the beach to see the midnight sun. The sun looked ready to set, but it didn't. Instead of disappearing, it began to rise once more. In the distance a wolf howled.

*That's a good omen,* Jean thought.

It was hard to sleep in the perpetual daylight, but they managed by pretending to take a nap. The next day they visited the Naval Arctic Research Laboratory to talk to several wolf experts.

One scientist had stayed up all night watching two wolves interact and monitoring their heart rates. Another, Dr. Michael Fox, led them to a wild wolf inside a cage. The male was gray, glistening and beautiful.

As Jean and Luke watched, the wolf approached Luke and sniffed through his cage. Then he walked to the opposite end of the cage, but turned, opening his mouth and showing his teeth.

"He likes you, Luke," Dr. Fox said. "He's smiling."

Dr. Fox explained that the wolf was friendly to Luke because he could tell he was a child, and, therefore, not a threat. Had Luke been a man, the wolf would have been afraid. The wolf wasn't afraid of Dr. Fox, however, because they were used to each other.

He explained about the many ways wolves communicate with one another: by voice, scent, eye contact, and body markings and movement. Wolves have their own language; they send messages by using a variety of whines, growls, barks, and howls. They're much like dogs in the way they use scent—when one wolf sniffs another, he can tell a lot about that wolf. Like dogs, wolves mark their territory by urinating. As for eye contact, wolves, like humans, send signals to each other this way, by looking each other in the eye.

Finally, Dr. Fox discussed the body language of wolves. Leaders hold their heads and tails high, while weak wolves hold their heads and tails low. Whenever a wolf shows his white belly, he is communicating, "I surrender." An alpha[2] wolf shows he's a leader by putting his mouth over the muzzles of other wolves. In return, the subordinate wolves then lick the alpha; some get down on their bellies or roll over.

Dr. Fox opened the door of the cage and stepped inside. He began to whine, then put his mouth on the wolf's nose. In wolf language, Dr. Fox was telling this wolf that *he* was the boss. Jean caught her breath, wondering whether the wolf would bite. But he licked the scientist, who then scratched his ears.

Jean couldn't believe it. Here was the supposedly wild wolf, feared by so many—yet he seemed as gentle as a cocker spaniel. At that moment she decided she had to learn their language.

Next Dr. Fox showed them a cage containing a mother and four pups, whom he was studying to learn about the personalities of alphas. He put a tin can inside, something the young wolves had never seen. Each one stared at the shiny new object, but only one came close and sniffed.

He was the alpha pup. Dr. Fox found that alphas are fearless, take initiative,[3] and possess great tenacity.[4]

After touring the rest of the lab, Jean returned to the mother wolf, whom she called Silver because of her light gray coat. Silver lay in one corner of the cage, surrounded by sleeping pups.

Jean whined, trying to imitate Dr. Fox. Silver didn't seem to notice. Jean tried again; this time Silver moved one eyebrow. Jean tried different noises, sounds she thought to be wolflike, but Silver drifted off to sleep.

The next day, Luke got to play with the pups, holding and cuddling them like pets. One of the scientists asked if Luke wanted to take one home; he assured them the wolf would make a good pet.

---

2. **alpha** lead; dominant

3. **initiative** responsibility; leadership

4. **tenacity** persistence; determination

He added: "If there was ever any doubt in my mind that a man could live with the wolves, it is gone now. The wolves are truly gentlemen, highly social and affectionate."

Jean didn't doubt his words, but knew it wouldn't be safe to take a puppy home. The problem was people—too many were afraid of wolves, and a pet wolf was likely to be shot.

On this and subsequent[5] visits, Jean continued to try to talk to Silver. She had little luck, until suddenly, during one visit, Silver curled her lips in a smile, looked Jean in the eye, and wagged her tail.

She had done it! Jean had talked to a wolf!

Silver continued to "talk," moving and making noises. Jean had no idea what the wolf was saying.

But when Silver tugged the sleeve of her coat, Jean thought she understood.

"You want me to come live with you?" she said. "I wish I could. But I can't."

With a little growl, Silver turned away.

Jean decided she wanted a parka from Alaska as a souvenir. That's how she and Luke met Julia Sevegan, a seamstress who also worked as a nurse's aide at the hospital in Barrow. Jean went to her home to be measured; Julia would make the parka and mail it to Jean in New York.

The Sevegans lived in a small house on the edge of the Arctic Ocean. Julia's workroom, which was also her bedroom and living room, was filled with a sewing machine, brightly colored scraps of fabric, and the furs of polar bears, caribou,[6] and seals. Guns, paddles, and harpoons hung on one wall—Julia's husband was a hunter.

Julia was a short woman with a round face, dark eyes, and black hair. Mr. Sevegan told Jean that she was a shaman, a person with magical healing powers.

When Jean asked about this, Julia responded, "It's because I once saw a ten-legged bear."

"That can't be," Jean said. "It must have been a mother with her cubs standing behind her."

"No," Julia said firmly, looking stern.

---

5. **subsequent**  following; coming later
6. **caribou**  large North American reindeer

Jean immediately wished she hadn't doubted her new acquaintance.[7] The awkwardness ended, however, when Luke said, "That's amazing!"

Julia smiled, then said she would show them a picture of the bear, which her son had drawn. She removed something from the wall that Jean recognized as baleen, the part of a whale's upper jawbone that serves as teeth. Scratched on the surface were a ten-legged polar bear, icebergs, and hunters.

"It *does* have ten legs," Jean said, trying to make amends.

Julia smiled and said, "Take it. It's an animal spirit."

Jean was surprised, and at first felt she shouldn't take such a special gift from someone she had just met. However, she understood that the people of Julia's culture had ideas different from her own, and that this was Julia's way of welcoming her and Luke.

"I'm honored," she said.

Julia measured Jean for the parka and decided on its design. It would take several months to make the handsome, red velvet coat trimmed with the fur of an Arctic fox.

At one point Julia looked at Luke and said, "If you lived according to our ancient traditions, you'd be married by now."

Luke's eyes widened. "Why?" he asked.

"Your parents would make arrangements with the parents of a girl, and you would go live in their igloo. You would hunt and work with the men. On the day that you killed your first caribou or seal, you would be considered a man, no longer a boy. But you would still stay with your wife's family. Later, the two of you would move back to your family's igloo. You wouldn't build your own igloo until you and your wife had learned to work well together as a team—you had become a good hunter and she had learned to make clothes and food. By then you would probably have children."

Luke frowned. He was glad *not* to be an Eskimo.

Before Jean and Luke left, Mr. Sevegan showed them the family freezer—a large, deep pit beside the house. A door protected the entrance; a ladder led to the bottom. This freezer required no electricity—permafrost kept all the meat frozen: caribou, reindeer, seal, duck, and whale.

---

7. **acquaintance** person whom one knows, but who is not a close friend

Walking back to the hotel, Jean told Luke, "Eskimos have to be incredibly smart to survive here."

Jean kept thinking about Julia and her husband. Both of them, she realized, were alphas, leaders. In this harsh environment, they couldn't survive without each other. Mr. Sevegan provided the food, while Julia cooked and made the clothes. Jean was full of admiration for both of them.

Early the next morning, Jean and Luke decided to explore the tundra. The landscape was strange, full of grass, moss, marshes, and lakes where the snow had melted. The view looked the same for miles in every direction.

Jean and Luke startled a huge flock of red-backed sandpipers; several thousand flapped into the air. They also saw Arctic terns, wondrous gull-like birds that migrate from the top of the world to the bottom and back again, between the Arctic and Antarctica, each year. They also saw a pair of snowy owls, one with a lemming in its beak. Luke had held one of these small Arctic rodents at the naval laboratory.

After about an hour, Jean and Luke turned around. It was time to go back. But a few minutes later, Luke said, "Mom, Barrow is behind us."

Jean stopped. "That can't be right," she said. "It must be a mirage."[8]

She was sure they were going in the right direction, that Barrow was straight ahead. She looked at the sun and the shadows. With the sun directly overhead, however, she could no longer rely on it as a compass. She knew how to navigate in the woods; she never got lost. But here in the Arctic, everything was different.

She climbed to the top of a frost heave[9] for a better view. Luke *was* right. Barrow was behind them, exactly opposite of where she thought it was. Suddenly Jean understood the stories she'd heard of hunters who become lost, walking in circles for days.

Changing direction, they walked toward the towers and rooftops of Barrow, trying to keep them in sight every step of the way. Jean was relieved to make it back safely.

Jean had heard about a man named Gordon Haber, a graduate

---

8. **mirage** optical illusion, something that appears real but is not
9. **frost heave** rise caused by frost displacing rocks or soil

student at McKinley National Park (now known as Denali National Park) who was studying wolf packs in the wild. The wolves here in the Barrow lab were fascinating, but they were caged, slightly "socialized" to the ways of humans. Jean wanted to see wolves running wild, completely free.

Before leaving Barrow, she and Luke paid a farewell visit to the lab. While Luke inspected a caged polar bear, Jean walked over to Silver's pen. She whimpered, but Silver deliberately ignored her. Wolf language can be very different from human ways of communicating. In wolf language, Silver's refusal to take notice meant she knew Jean was there and that she mattered.

Only when another wolf howled, did Silver respond more directly, sitting up and howling. One by one, all the wolves in the lab began to sing their eerie song.

Once in the shadows of the mighty Mount McKinley, Jean and Luke spent hours listening to Haber, who had been studying wild wolf packs for nearly five years. He camped outside near their dens from April through November, following their movements and learning their ways.

For more than a week, Jean and Luke camped on the banks of the Sanctuary River. They didn't have a tent, so they spread their sleeping bags underneath a spruce.

Haber took them to an observation site he had established above a wolf den. Jean and Luke peered at the wolves through a telescope. The scientist didn't want them to get any closer; he feared they might scare the wolves away.

As Jean caught a glimpse of the black alpha, Haber explained that this male made all the decisions. Alphas grew bigger than the other wolves for reasons no one understood. Jean couldn't help giving this animal a name—Amaroq—the Inupiat word for wolf. Jean watched him eat, play, sleep, and keep order among the group.

One evening Amaroq raised his head, closed his eyes, and began to howl—the hunt song. The alpha female joined in, then the rest, in order of status. Amaroq and two other adults set off single file, leaving the young in the care of a "babysitter" wolf. The pups immediately began to romp; one of their favorite games was "jump-on-the-babysitter."

Very early one morning, Haber awakened Jean and Luke, inviting them to accompany him to the pack's previous den, known as the "nursery den," where the pups had been born. He held a large rifle.

"What's that for?" Jean asked.

"Grizzlies."

Jean was worried. With so few trees, there was no place to hide on the tundra, and a ranger had spotted several bears near the nursery, three miles away. But she wanted to see the den.

Once there, Jean relaxed. The den, which was located on a ridge above the river, had a spectacular view—and was the perfect place to watch for bears. They could see for miles: canyons, rocks, snow-topped mountains, and clouds. Sometimes, when the clouds lifted, they caught a glimpse of Mount McKinley. Wildflowers grew all around. Jean wished she had her paints.

The wolves had left signs of their presence. There were holes where the pups had learned to dig. The adults had molded the ground into "sleeping cups." The den itself consisted of a tunnel and chamber.

Just as they were leaving, Jean gazed into the distance, overcome by the beauty. That's when she saw it—a huge bear. It wasn't too close, but it was heading toward the trail they would be using. Jean knew that although bears look clumsy, they can run fast—as swiftly as 40 miles per hour.

"Grizzly!" she shouted. She crouched down, ready to hide.

"Come on!" Haber shouted. "We've got to run. We have to get ahead of him."

They had a lightning-quick discussion. Jean and Luke's first in- stinct was to stay put until the bear was gone. Haber said that if they didn't get ahead of him, they would have to walk behind him on the same trail. The bear might turn around and catch their scent. Jean and Luke decided to follow Haber's advice.

Haber and Luke started running. Jean followed, but her feet felt like lead. The tundra was tough terrain, spongy and uneven, and Jean felt like she was moving slowly. But after she passed a flying jay, she knew she was making good time.

When Jean caught up with him, Haber stopped and looked back. The bear had turned around. They were out of danger.

As they gasped for breath, a wolf began to howl. The sound came from the den they had just fled. A female and her pups were standing on the ridge, watching them suspiciously. Jean shivered. Here, on the turf of wolves and grizzlies, humans were uninvited visitors.

That night, as they thought about their encounter with the bear, Jean and Luke took longer than usual to fall asleep. Jean heard the wolves howling, then drifted off thinking how each member of the pack had an important role to play, how each one depended on the others for survival—just as Julia and her husband depended on each other.

Their trip would soon be over. She couldn't wait to write her article.

Sylvia A.
Johnson and
Alice Aamodt

# Killing to Survive

## from *Wolf Pack: Tracking Wolves in the Wild*

*As carnivores—not herbivores or omnivores—wolves have to hunt every bite of food they eat. Authors Sylvia Johnson and Alice Aamodt explain how and what wolves hunt. They also examine the role the pack plays in the life of a wolf.*

EVEN UNDER NORMAL CIRCUMSTANCES, survival is not easy for wolves in the wild. Their lives as predators are difficult, and they often go hungry for days, even weeks, at a time. Although wolves are skillful hunters, they face many obstacles in their search for prey. Only their ability to act as a group makes it possible for them to feed themselves and their young.

Wolves are *carnivores*, or meat-eaters, and hunting is a year-round activity for a wolf pack. In winter snow or summer heat, pack members must search for the prey animals on which their diet depends. A pack's hunting schedule varies somewhat, however, depending on the time of year.

During the spring and summer, all the pack's activities are controlled by the presence of the pups and the need to guard and care for them. For the few weeks that the pups are in the den with the mother wolf, the other pack members go out to hunt, usually at night, and return to the den site the next day.

When the pups are 8 to 10 weeks old and able to leave the den, they are moved to a *rendezvous site* within the pack's territory. A rendezvous site is just what the name suggests; it is a meeting place for pack members as well as a home base for the pups. While their relatives are out on their nightly round of hunting, the pups stay at the site with an adult "pupsitter." The hunters return each morning with food for the young and then spend the day resting or playing at the rendezvous site. A pack usually uses one site for two or three weeks before moving the pups to a different spot, probably to be closer to prey animals.

The autumn and winter schedule of a wolf pack is quite different. By this time of year, the pups are at least six months old and capable of traveling with the adult wolves, although at a somewhat slower pace. Now the pack is on the move day and night, stopping only for periods of rest, play, and feeding. The group has no permanent or even semi-permanent headquarters but rambles throughout its territory, following the trails of the animals on which it preys.

Just what these prey animals are depends on the part of the world in which the pack lives. In general, however, most wolves hunt hooved mammals like moose, deer, caribou, elk, and mountain sheep. Wolves are able to take these large animals because they hunt in groups, combining their strength and cunning[1] to catch and kill their prey. A wolf hunting alone is able to capture animals like beavers, rabbits, hares, mice, and birds. Most of these smaller creatures, however, make only a mouthful for a hungry wolf. In order to feed its many members, a pack must be able to bring down large prey.

Locating prey is the first big job of hunting wolves. During their daily or nightly travels, the predators are always alert for signs that prey animals are nearby. Most frequently, the signs are in the form of scents picked up from the air by the wolves' sensitive noses. If the wind is blowing from the direction of the prey animals toward the wolves, the predators are able to smell the odor as much as a mile and a half away. Wolves can also use their sense of smell to follow the fresh tracks of animals on the ground, although wind-borne odors more often lead them to their prey.

When a pack of wolves picks up the scent of prey, the animals become very excited and alert. They sniff the air and then set off in the direction of their quarry,[2] moving swiftly but cautiously. Their goal is

---

1. **cunning** slyness
2. **quarry** animal that is being hunted

to get close to the prey without revealing their presence, so silence and speed are essential.

If they succeed in their quest, the wolves dash toward the animal, surround it, and bring it down by biting its rump, sides, neck, and head. In most cases, death comes quickly, and the predators begin to tear at the prey's flesh with their strong teeth, pulling off large pieces and bolting them down with very little chewing. By the time they are done, nothing will be left of the animal but the stomach contents (the remains of plant food, not to the taste of these meat-eaters), hooves, and perhaps some of the largest bones. The wolves eat everything else.

If the prey animals pick up the scent of the wolves or see them approaching, then the hunt may have a different outcome. The animals may escape by running, or they may stand and try to defend themselves against the predators' attack. Both methods have saved many potential prey from becoming a meal for a wolf pack.

Deer and caribou, which are also members of the deer family, are swift runners and, given half a chance, can escape from a pursuing wolf pack. The larger, heavier moose is not so fleet,[3] but with a head-start, it can also get away from the predators. Wolves will chase a running animal for only so long. If they cannot quickly close the gap between themselves and their prey, they will usually give up the chase and look for an easier quarry. Wolves are very practical predators, and they seem to have a good sense of how much energy they should expend in pursuing prey. If the exertion[4] of a long-distance chase would take more energy than would be gained from eating the object of the chase, then it is not worth the effort.

Hunting wolves can also be thwarted[5] by a prey animal that puts up a vigorous self-defense. Moose are particularly successful in using this method of escape. If an adult moose is pursued by a wolf pack, it will sometimes stand and face its attackers instead of running. A full-grown male moose weighs as much as 1,250 pounds (about 560 kilograms) and has a massive set of antlers on its head. In defending itself, a moose will try to gore[6] an attacking wolf with its antlers or kick the

---

3. **fleet**  swift; fast
4. **exertion**  effort
5. **thwarted**  hindered; frustrated; defeated
6. **gore**  pierce

predator with its heavy hooves. Faced with this kind of resistance, wolves will often give up the attack.

Because prey animals have so many avenues of escape, wolves do not have a very high success rate in their careers as hunters. Observers have estimated that less than 10 percent of a pack's attempts to catch prey end successfully.

Luckily, wolves have a great capacity to go without food for long periods of time. They can survive for as much as two weeks without eating. When food is available, they gorge[7] themselves to make up for the periods of famine. Adult wolves are capable of eating as much as 20 pounds (about 14 kilograms) of meat at one time.

When wolves are successful in taking prey, the animals they kill are usually not mature, healthy adults. Adult deer, caribou, and moose in good condition are able to escape the predators in most situations by fleeing or defending themselves. The animals that cannot escape are usually the very young, the old, and the diseased.

Young deer, moose, and caribou are not able to run as quickly as the adults, and they are incapable of defending themselves. During the spring and summer, a wolf pack's diet is made up largely of deer fawns or moose and caribou calves whose mothers have not been able to protect them from the predators' attacks.

At other times of year, when there is not such a large supply of young prey, wolves seem to concentrate on the old and sick. Weakened by age or by the ravages[8] of diseases and parasites,[9] these animals too do not have the strength and speed needed to avoid the predators' sharp teeth.

From the human point of view, it might seem "unfair" of wolves to take advantage of their prey's weakness in this way. Of course, human standards of fairness have no meaning in the natural world. Wolves must have food in order to live, and they get it in the way that is easiest for them, taking the least expenditure of energy and producing the greatest return.

From this point of view, killing and eating young, old, and sick prey animals makes a great deal of sense. Surprisingly enough, it usually makes sense in terms of the prey's welfare too, at least when the

---

7. **gorge**  eat greedily
8. **ravages**  devastating damage
9. **parasites**  organisms that live on or in organisms of a different species, usually with harmful effects

group rather than the individual is considered. If wolves kill the old and sick caribou in a herd, then the younger, healthier members of the group will have more food, less chance of catching diseases, and a better chance of surviving. The health of the group will also be improved because these unfit animals will not be able to produce offspring that might inherit their unhealthy condition.

But what about wolves killing the young? How could that "heartless" slaughter possibly benefit a group of prey animals? In many situations, it does just that by controlling the size of the prey population in a particular area. A smaller population means more food for the survivors and, again, better health and living conditions for the group as a whole.

Of course, the relationship between wolves and their prey is not often so simple. Its delicate balance can be affected by many different factors, including human interference.

For example, in areas where the natural food supply of deer or moose has been damaged by severe weather or by human activities, populations of these plant-eating creatures will gradually decline. If wolves live in the area, they may bring about a further decline by preying on the remaining animals. This combination of destructive factors could eventually reduce the population drastically, perhaps to the point where the deer or moose are eliminated from the region. If this happens, the wolves too will be affected since their survival depends on an adequate supply of prey animals.

When the animals they prey on are gone, wolves either have to leave the area or look for another source of food. Sometimes they find an alternate source in the form of domestic animals—cattle, sheep, and other creatures confined on farms and ranches. If wild prey is not available, wolves will attack and kill domestic animals. The predators must have meat to survive, and of course, they do not recognize the fact that such animals are the property of human beings.

When wolves attack domestic animals, they sometimes behave differently than they do when killing wild prey. In the wild, wolves normally kill only what they need for food and they eat almost all of a prey animal. When domestic creatures are on the menu, however, the predators may kill many more animals than they can eat. They may consume only small portions of their prey and leave the carcasses[10] almost untouched.

---

10. **carcasses** bodies of dead animals

This "overkill" happens most frequently when wolves attack a large number of animals confined in a pen or a fenced area. Other predators such as wild cats also exhibit the same behavior in similar situations. Scientist believe that such abnormal behavior is produced by a kind of "short-circuit" in the predators' hunting instincts.

In the wild, killing is part of a whole set of instinctive[11] actions that include searching for the prey, stalking and chasing it, and finally bringing it down and eating it. When predators are confronted by a group of domestic animals unable to run or to defend themselves, they are stimulated to perform only one part of the hunting sequence—the kill. They may kill again and again because the prey is available in large numbers and easy to catch, a situation that rarely exists in a natural setting.

Farmers and ranchers are understandably upset when wolves attack their animals in this way. In this situation as in so many others, however, the wolves are blamed for a problem that they did not create, a problem that exists because human activities have interfered with the predators' natural way of life. Such blame has frequently been part of the human attitude toward wolves. The troubled relationship between wolves and people has a very long history, most of which does little credit to the understanding or good sense of the human race.

---

11. **instinctive** natural; unlearned

Jean Craighead
George

# from
# *Julie's Wolf Pack*

*This excerpt from the sequel to* Julie of the Wolves
*tells of Kapu's dominance in the pack and of the end
of the famine that threatens the wolves' existence.*

THE WOLVES OF THE AVALIK RIVER ran in and out among the
musk oxen.[1] Their ruffs[2] rippled like banners. Ice crystals danced up
from their feet. The pack swirled like a twist of wind-blown snow.
Their yellow eyes flashed and dimmed in the coming and going of the
ice mist. Like the snow, they made no sound.

The musk oxen stopped and stared at the enemy. Then they lowered
their shaggy heads and pawed down to the new grass growing under the
snow. Their breath rose in steamy clouds and froze on their brows.

Kapu, the young leader of the wolf pack, reared on his hind legs,
leaped to point the way, and led his clan to a turquoise-blue rise on
the treeless Arctic tundra.

He carried himself proudly, with his chest forward and his head
high. His black fur was brushed to a shine by the wind. His body was
strongly muscled. He was the leader of the wolf pack that had saved
the life of the young Eskimo girl, Miyax—whose English name was
Julie Edwards—when she was lost on the Arctic tundra. She, in turn,
had saved them by leading them to a new food source during the great
caribou[3] famine.[4] The Yupik and Iñupiat Eskimos of Kangik called
them "Julie's wolf pack."

---

1. **musk oxen** wild oxen that live in the far north
2. **ruffs** protruding fur around the necks of animals
3. **caribou** large deer of the tundra; reindeer
4. **famine** shortage of food

Kapu was keenly aware of Julie. She was not far away. He whisked his tail. She had read his message to the oxen, for she was no longer afraid that he would kill one. The villagers collected the wool from these sturdy animals to weave into light, warm clothing, and they zealously[5] protected them.

"We are not hunting you," Kapu had said to the oxen with his body movements. "We chase you for the joy of it. We are wolves of the caribou."

Kapu and his followers were having fun. The shaggy herd deciphered[6] this and returned to their grazing. Julie deciphered it and told her father, Kapugen. He chuckled and slipped his arm around her shoulders. The two walked quietly home.

Kapu wagged his tail. Chasing the oxen was a fine wolf joke. His rime-gray[7] mate, Aaka, playfully spanked the ground with her forepaws, her rear end in the air. Zing—the beta, or second in command—enjoyed the joke even more than Kapu. His breathing came faster, and the pupils of his eyes enlarged ever so slightly. He smiled by lifting his lips from his glistening teeth. Pearly-white Silver, Kapu's mother, and her ill-tempered new mate, Raw Bones, also smiled. But Amy, Kapu's night-black daughter, did not get the joke. She was not old enough to know that her pack preferred caribou to musk oxen. Nor did she know that some packs harvest only deer and ignore moose, or harvest moose and caribou and ignore deer. Others take elk; a few take musk oxen. When the Avalik River Pack had a choice, they were wolves of the caribou. Wolves have their cultures.[8]

The adolescent Amy studied the curled horns and bony brows of the musk oxen, then looked at her regal[9] father. If he thought the chase was fun, then she did, too. She wagged her tail.

Amy could not possibly know that her pack were caribou wolves. She had been born in a caribou famine. These big Arctic deer had failed to come to Avalik territory for many years. The pack had taken what food they could find—a musk ox killed by a grizzly bear, rabbits,

---

5. **zealously**  fervently; enthusiastically
6. **deciphered**  translated
7. **rime-gray**  encrusted with frost or ice granules
8. **cultures**  ways of doing things
9. **regal**  king-like; royal

lemmings.[10] Late in the fall they were able to add an occasional moose to their diet, but by March of her first year Amy's pack was starving again. The moose were gone. The wolves grew thin. They tired easily. When the breeding season arrived that month, her parents did not mate. Aaka, her mother, was undernourished. There had not been enough food for her to develop healthy puppies.

The rangy, self-important Raw Bones knew well that the pack had not had enough to eat for years. Nevertheless, he approached Silver to start their family. Kapu rushed to him. Hair rising on his back, ears erect and pointed forward, Kapu talked to him in the wolf language of posturing. Then he lifted his head above him and rumbled a dark authoritative growl that said plainly, "No pups." It is inherent[11] in the leader of the wolf pack that he uses his judgment and makes such a decision. Raw Bones ignored him. He stepped closer to Silver.

Kapu bared his teeth and drew the corners of his mouth forward. His forehead wrinkled.

Raw Bones challenged this reprimand[12] with a jaw snap. Kapu grabbed the back of his neck but did not clamp down with his bone-crushing jaws. He did not need to. He was saying, "I am the leader. No pups." Raw Bones drew his ears back and close to his head. He pulled his tail between his legs and lowered his body. This posture said, "You are the leader. I submit to you."

Obediently Raw Bones slunk off to the edge of the pack in the manner of a chastised[13] wolf citizen. But he did not mean it.

He glanced back to see if Kapu was looking at him. If not, he would sneak-attack him. Kapu was looking. He displayed one canine tooth. It shone lethal white against the black of his lips. "Don't dare," it said. Raw Bones lay down. Rumbling sounds of peevishness[14] rolled in his chest. He did not like being dominated,[15] especially by a younger male.

Kapu did not completely relax. Raw Bones was his rival. He

---

10. **lemmings**  small rodents
11. **inherent**  natural; inborn; unlearned
12. **reprimand**  rebuke; scolding
13. **chastised**  scolded
14. **peevishness**  irritation; impatience
15. **dominated**  ruled

wanted to be leader of the Avaliks, Kapu's pack. He had been alpha[16] male wolf of the Upper Colville River Pack for many years. Then the famine struck. One by one the members of his pack starved to death until he was the only one left alive. When his new mate, Silver, joined him, they survived on rabbits and other small mammals and waited for the famine to end and the feasting to begin. Feast and famine are the natural rhythm of the Arctic tundra. The caribou eat themselves out of grasses and moss and move to greener lands. The wolves adjust. Many die. The alpha males and females have few or no pups. Then time heals. Without the caribou to crop them, the grasses and mosses spring up in abundance. The caribou return. The wolves feast and have pups again. This has been the rhythm of nature for the past 500,000 years.

Raw Bones and Silver waited for the cycle to end by sleeping long hours to conserve energy. They were curled tightly, saving body heat, when the Avaliks arrived at the border of their own property across the river. Between Kapu's and Raw Bones's territories was a broad corridor[17] into which neither pack would go. It was the no-wolf zone, an area fenced off with howls and scent marks to keep wolf packs from fighting and killing each other.

Silver heard a wolf voice beyond the no-wolf zone. She lifted her head. Kapu, her son, was calling, "Come hunt with us," communicating in the wolf language of song.

She jumped up, eager to join him. Relatives can cross the no-wolf zone when invited. She trotted toward the river. Raw Bones held back. He had been trained all his life not to enter these corridors. Adolescents leaving home to look for a new pack, and lone wolves, can hide in them, but not leaders. Not Raw Bones.

Yet he had heard Kapu's invitation. Invitations are important in wolf protocol.[18] He arose. A raging hunger and the scent knowledge that Kapu was Silver's son urged him slowly forward.

Silver took a deep draft of air. The perfume of Willow Pup Julie was on it. She wagged her tail. The human cub who had joined her family long ago was coming her way.

Willow Pup Julie appeared among the knobby alder trees. She

---

16. **alpha** socially dominant, especially in a group of animals
17. **corridor** strip of land
18. **protocol** set of rules governing communication

carried Kapu's invitation in the odors on her clothes. Silver pranced a wolf dance of survival. By joining the Avaliks, she would live. She ran to the river. Raw Bones was reluctant but understood what he must do. Head down, he skirted Willow Pup and splashed into the river behind Silver. They crossed to the forbidden land.

The packs met. Stiff-legged, nervous, they greeted each other with mouth sniffs and brief tail whisks. All tails curved downward and cricked in suspicion, then each hung loose and relaxed to tell the other wolves they would cooperate and hunt together. Antlered animals with their sharp hoofs are violent prey. The more wolves, the better.

But it was not that simple. There can be but one alpha male and one alpha female leading a pack. Kapu and Raw Bones snapped at each other, testing to see which it would be. They were both leaders. The battle for rank began as they lifted their tails. Then each inhaled the other's scent and learned of his health, vigor,[19] and dominance. Finally each growled his lowest note. Raw Bones was older. This gave him the advantage. He raised his head above Kapu's to say he was boss. Kapu would not tolerate it. He threw Raw Bones to the ground. Raw Bones quickly got to his feet. Kapu lifted his head above Raw Bones's. Both wrinkled their brows and curled back their black lips to show gleaming white fangs. Growling, they threatened each other. Raw Bones tried to get his paw on Kapu's back, but Kapu kept his head and chest above him. He snarled deep and low. With that the battle was over. Not a drop of blood was spilled. Kapu had won.

This was an important victory for the young wolf leader. Upon the death of his father, Amaroq, he had taken over the leadership of the pack. The death of an alpha male wolf is a tragedy, like the death of a nation's president. For the wolves it takes many years to make a leader as strong and knowledgeable as Amaroq had been. Kapu did not have time to develop with Raw Bones in his pack. To survive, he had to be dominant now. He had the fearlessness and initiative of an alpha, but he was young. That is a disadvantage when confronted with an older wolf. By sheer bravado,[20] by snarling and growling and keeping his head above Raw Bones's, Kapu had held on to his rank as alpha male wolf of the Avaliks.

---

19. **vigor** strength; energy
20. **bravado** pretended courage or confidence

Raw Bones did not like it. He would try again.

Leadership settled for the moment, the six wolves worked together that early-autumn season, hunting the moose that had been protected for years in the no-wolf zone. At first they fared well; then the moose became scarce. Grizzlies and human hunters were also harvesting them.

The famine went on. The caribou did not migrate south through Avalik land in the late fall. The wolves lost weight and vigor.

In March, the breeding month, Kapu made the decision for himself and Aaka as well as for Silver and Raw Bones not to have pups.

Many sleeps later, his sensitive ears picked up the sounds he had been waiting for: the snorts and bleats of the western Arctic caribou herd. The pregnant females had left the forest and were migrating by the tens of thousands to their calving grounds on the tundra. The bulls and adolescents would follow later.

As the murmur swelled into a drone,[21] Kapu paced the riverbank. He mapped the course of the herd using his senses—smell, taste, sight, sound, and, through the pads of his feet, touch. He paced faster. The caribou were in the territory of the Mountain Pack. They were crossing creek beds eating willows, star gentians, and butterworts. Then they were trotting through Raw Bones's old territory and approaching the Colville River.

Would the herd go east, as it had for so many years, or come back to the grassy Avalik territory? The beta wolf, Zing, Kapu's faithful brother, trotted behind him waiting to be told what to do.

The sun set. The sky grew blue-purple, and the moon, a feeble glow by day, shone like a lamp.

Kapu tensed. He heard the musical click made by the tendons in the legs of the caribou snapping against bones as they walked—a sound only caribou make. He judged the herd to be in the Colville River valley. The river was deep in some places, shallow in others as it braided its way amid stunted alders and grass to the Arctic Ocean. Kapu waited.

The moon set. In the darkness the river gurgled and boiled. Two miles of caribou were throwing themselves into the deeper waters of the Colville and swimming. Others were splashing across the shallows.

---

21. **drone** continuous deep, monotonous sound

Two hours later the moon came up. Like the Arctic sun, the Arctic moon has its long night or long day. In the deep of winter the moon does not set. The sun, on the other hand, does not rise from late November until late January—the long Arctic night. It does not set from early May until early August—the long Arctic day.

In the pale moonlight of March, Kapu—who, like all wolves, could see in the dark as well as in the day—saw a tide of movement. He stopped pacing. The smell of trodden grass and moss filled his nose—his grass, his moss. The western Arctic herd was on Avalik land.

He lowered his haunches, threw back his head, and howled. His canyon-deep voice climbed an octave and faded. He repeated this song of celebration. Aaka sang a note and slid up the musical scale to harmonize with Kapu. Zing glided up to a note lower than Aaka's. Raw Bones found a note below Aaka's. Silver harmonized with him. They howled a chord of harmonizing notes that rose and fell and rose again. Their music gave the wolverines pause. The Arctic foxes listened. Amy was quiet for the first half of the song; then she began howling low and soared up to take a silver note above Kapu's. The princess of the Avaliks had made her debut.

The song ended abruptly. The caribou thundered up the riverbank and out across the tundra. The Avaliks melted into them, gliding quietly like shadows. The caribou paid them no heed. They were bound for their ancestral calving grounds.

Kapu, with faithful Zing at his shoulder, sped into the mass of caribou and split off a small group. He chased along beside them, watching for an animal to stumble or dash off alone in terror.

The isolated group sensed the wolves and put on speed. All were too swift and healthy for the wolves to catch. Kapu did not mind. The caribou were back. With no pups to keep his pack members at the den, he could lead his pack north to the calving grounds and harvest the weak and sick caribou. The Avaliks would become stronger and stronger, and Kapu would grow in wisdom and experience until he was as grand as his father, and Raw Bones would forever be subdued.[22]

The birth of wolf pups in late May and early June is well timed for both prey and predator. When the female caribou are dropping their calves, the wolves are at their dens raising pups. This gives the calves

---

22. **subdued** conquered; controlled

six weeks or more to grow and develop their running skills. As for the wolves, it is to their advantage not to prey on the calves. A herd could be wiped out by overharvesting the helpless young.

But this year Kapu had changed the biological plan. No pups. He and his wolves would travel right into the midst of the calving grounds and regain their strength and vigor during the summer. They would eat well. Next year, when they were healthy and strong, they would have super pups. Only super wolf pups can survive in the wilderness.

**Rebecca Stefoff**

# from
# *Celebrate the States: Alaska*

*If you could cut Alaska out of a map and place it on top of a map of the forty-eight mainland states, the eastern edge of the panhandle would cover South Carolina and Georgia, and the western islands would reach into California. Rebecca Stefoff tells more about the largest state in the United States.*

WHEN THE FIRST WHITE PEOPLE came to Alaska, they met the Aleuts. These Native people lived on a string of islands at the end of a long finger of land stretching out into the sea. To the east was the mainland, which the Aleuts called Alyeska (al-YES-ka). This old Aleut name is often said to mean "the great land."

Alaska *is* a great land, in more ways than one. "This is the Last Frontier, a land of gold rushes and bush pilots, of blue glaciers and snowy mountains, of the oil pipeline and bountiful[1] salmon," a traveler named Matt Nauman wrote excitedly during his first visit to Alaska. He wanted to see the "real Alaska"—but he soon realized that he couldn't hope to see it all. Alaska is simply too big.

## The Biggest State

The single most important fact about Alaska, the thing that astounds every visitor and shapes the life of every resident, is the size of the place. It is one-fifth the size of the rest of the nation and two-and-a-half times as large as Texas. Its coastline is longer than all the coastlines of the rest of the United States added together.

---

1. **bountiful** abundant; plentiful

This state is not just big, it's also filled with big things. Alaska has the highest mountain in North America: Mount Denali, also called McKinley, which is 20,320 feet high. It has the country's largest national park, Wrangell-Saint Elias (13 million acres); its largest national forest, Tongass (50,000 square miles); and its largest state park, Wood-Tikchik (1.6 million acres). Alaska has the world's longest chain of active volcanoes. It has more glaciers, or moving ice fields, than the rest of the inhabited world, and the biggest ones are larger than the state of Rhode Island. Even Alaska's natural disasters are huge. The most powerful recorded earthquake in North American history rocked central Alaska in 1964.

The second key fact about Alaska is that, like Hawaii, it is separated from the rest of the United States. Alaska is bordered on the north by the Arctic Ocean and on the south by the Gulf of Alaska and Pacific Ocean. To the west are the Bering Sea and Chukchi Sea, with Russia on the other side. At their closest point, Russia and Alaska are only fifty-one miles apart. To the east is Canada. Alaskans call the rest of the continental United States, below Canada, the Lower Forty-eight.

## Five Regions

Alaska is shaped roughly like a square standing on two legs. One leg is the panhandle,[2] which runs southeast along the coast of Canada. The other is the Alaska Peninsula, which stretches southwest and then breaks up into a 1,600-mile-long chain of islands called the Aleutians—the home of the Aleuts. The state's five geographic regions are the southeast, the south central, the southwest, the interior, and the far north.

### Southeast

Alaska's southeastern panhandle is a region of water and land, a narrow strip of islands, inlets, and peninsulas. The Inside Passage is a waterway that threads among the islands, sheltering ships from the storms of the open northern sea. To the east, the Coast Mountains march along the passage in snowcapped majesty.

"This place is like a picture from a calendar or something," said tourist Martine Wirley, watching from the deck of a cruise ship as the

---

2. **panhandle** strip of land projecting like the handle of a pan

morning fog lifted. Ahead, a ribbon of silver water wound between dozens of islands carpeted with dark green spruce and hemlock trees. "It's the most peaceful place I've ever seen."

## South Central

At the top of the panhandle, the Coast Range gives way to the rugged Saint Elias Mountains, marking the beginning of south-central Alaska, a region of mountains, glaciers, forests, lakes, and streams. This steep and dramatic landscape was shaped by huge ice sheets that carved deep, narrow valleys during ice ages many thousands of years ago.

The Saint Elias, Chugach, and Talkeetna Mountains follow the coast. A little inland are the Wrangell Mountains. Still farther inland sweeps the Alaska Range. Many of the mountains are volcanoes, part of the "Ring of Fire" that encircles the Pacific Ocean. These ranges also contain most of the state's 29,000 square miles of glaciers. Some glaciers cling to high mountain slopes, while others flow like sluggish rivers of ice through the valleys. The spectacular tidewater glaciers drop into the sea.

At the middle of the southern coast is the Kenai Peninsula. The Kenai Mountains run the length of the peninsula. On either side are huge, deep inlets of the sea: Prince William Sound on the east and Cook Inlet on the west.

## Southwest

Southwestern Alaska begins at the long Alaska Peninsula, with the Aleutian Mountains as its backbone. These mountains seethe and hiss with volcanic life. Mount Pavlof, near the end of the peninsula, has erupted more than forty times since 1760. The biggest recorded eruption in Alaska occurred here in June of 1912, when a volcano in what is now Katmai National Park hurled so much ash into the air that skies were dark over most of the northern hemisphere for several days.

Lake Iliamna in the southwest covers 1,150 square miles and is the largest of the state's three million lakes. Kodiak Island, at 3,588 square miles, is the second-largest island in the United States, after Hawaii. Farther west are broad plains, sprinkled with lakes, where the Yukon and Kuskokwim Rivers meet the sea.

The Aleutian Islands trail out to sea "like the tail on a kite," says

Dan Grindling. These hilly, grass-covered islands are remote and not easy to reach, but they have a rugged beauty all their own. Abi Woodbridge owns a gift shop in Unalaska, the largest city in the islands. "There's something magical about this place," Woodbridge says. "When I came here in 1974, I just knew I was home."

## Interior

The interior of Alaska is bordered on the south by the towering Alaska Range, where Mount Denali rises. Beyond the Alaska Range are the Kuskokwim, Kaiyuh, Ray, and White Ranges. These mountains are low and weathered,[3] giving the land a broad, rolling appearance. The Yukon River, which flows across the interior from the Canadian border to the Yukon Delta, is the third-longest river in the United States, after the Mississippi and the Missouri. Its course cuts through a low-lying region called the Yukon Flats, covered with moist, boggy[4] terrain called muskeg.

## Far North

Alaska's far north begins with the Seward Peninsula and the Brooks Range. The Seward Peninsula is a broad, mostly treeless arm of land reaching toward Russia. The Brooks Range is a series of mountain ranges that separates Alaska's interior from the North Slope, a broad plain that runs down to the Arctic Ocean. Part of the peninsula and all of the North Slope are tundra, a generally flat landscape covered with tough mosses and hardy grasses. The only trees that grow in the tundra look more like low shrubs. Willow trees are only a few inches tall!

Several feet beneath the ground's surface is permafrost, frozen soil that never thaws and cannot absorb water. During the brief northern summer, surface water forms a web of lakes and ponds across the tundra, which blazes with the brilliant colors of short-lived wildflowers. People who live here build their houses on posts. Otherwise, the warmth from the houses would melt the permafrost, turning the tundra to mud, and the houses would sink. Even with the posts, the ground under a tundra house can get soggy. Some families have to move their houses every few years.

---

3. **weathered**  worn down by weather
4. **boggy**  spongy

## Rain, Snow, and Wind

"Alaska's almost big enough to be a continent in itself," says a weather reporter in Anchorage, in the south-central region. "We have half a dozen different climates. The south coast is as different from the north coast as Texas is from Minnesota."

Southern Alaska has a maritime climate, meaning that the sea keeps temperatures from becoming extremely hot or cold. The far north is the coldest region all year round. The interior of Alaska sees the most extreme changes in temperature. The lowest *and* highest temperatures ever recorded in Alaska came from the interior: –80 degrees Fahrenheit at Prospect Creek Camp in 1971, and 100 degrees at Fort Yukon in 1915. The people of Fairbanks, the biggest city of the interior, have learned to make the best of their harsh weather. Every March they hold an Ice Art Festival. Artists carve huge chunks of ice into dragons, mermaids, and other shapes all around town.

"To tell you about how cold it can get in Alaska," says Jerry Jacka, who used to live in Fairbanks, "one day I bought groceries and accidentally left the bananas in the car. That night the temperature dropped to 30 degrees below zero. The next morning the bananas were hard as rocks, and when I tapped them together they sounded like some sort of musical instrument. I made banana bread out of them and have had a beautiful singing voice ever since. Well, that last line is a little bit of an exaggeration, but most stories from Alaska are."

The panhandle gets a lot of rain but little snow except in the mountains. In contrast, snow blankets much of the interior during winter. The North Slope receives less, but there the biting wind molds the snow into deep drifts. High winds are an Alaskan weather hazard. Alaskans even have special names for their winds. Williwaws are sudden, unexpected gusts. Takus are bitterly cold, fast winds that rush down from ice caps high in the mountains onto southeastern communities. Chinooks are fast, warm winter winds that thaw ice and snow, destroy homes, and knock down power lines.

## Day and Night

Alaska is sometimes called the Land of the Midnight Sun. The farther north you go in summertime, the longer the days and the shorter the nights. The Arctic Circle marks the point where the sun doesn't set at all on the longest day of summer. North of the Arctic Circle, the sun stays in the sky for days at a time. In Barrow, on the north coast, the sun rises on May 10 and doesn't set until August 2, eighty-four days later. Many northern communities celebrate the midnight sun of summer. The people of Nome, for example, hold a midsummer festival that includes a softball tournament, races for rafts and mountain bikes, a barbecued-chicken feast, and a pie-eating contest.

For every long summer day, however, there comes a long winter night. During the winter, northern days get shorter and nights get longer. At the Arctic Circle, the sun doesn't rise at all on the shortest day of the year. In Barrow, the sun sets on November 18 and doesn't rise until January 24. "Land of the Midnight Sun sounds good," says Anita Rees, who lives in a cabin in the interior, "but Alaska could just as truly be called Land of the Dark Noon."

Some Alaskans suffer from cabin fever, feelings of restlessness or sadness during the long, dark winters when people spend most of their time indoors. Tempers can wear thin by spring. Governor Tony Knowles has said, "April is one tough month. Expectations rise as spring approaches, but if it stays cold or snows in April, people find that spring hasn't provided a cure-all. They go crazy." Says Harold Weaver, a newspaper editor in Anchorage, "Some people can't handle the cold and the dark. They come alive again when they can shake off their cabin fever."

| Gail B. Stewart | # Two Inches Above the Television Screen |
|---|---|

## from *Life in an Eskimo Village*

AT FIRST GLANCE, they could be teenagers from any American city. Some carry boom boxes, others chat about a new rock video they have seen on MTV. A few have dyed their hair orange or pink; others wear their hair more conservatively. Almost all of them are wearing jeans and T-shirts with familiar designs—Nike, Hard Rock Cafe, Grateful Dead.

But a closer look would reveal that these teenagers are different. Although their homes have satellite dishes to pull in cable TV, few of them have flush toilets or running water. None of the teenagers' families owns an automobile, but all have at least one snowmobile parked outside the front door. And besides pizza and hamburgers, these teenagers frequently eat seal meat for dinner . . .

### The World's Most Hostile Environment

These young people are Eskimos, living near or within the Arctic Circle. In the Canadian Arctic, they are known as Inupiat or Inuit; in western Alaska they are Yupik. Some Eskimos live in Greenland and Siberia. But no matter where Eskimos live, they are alike in one important respect—their homelands are scattered across the most hostile environment on earth.

In the Far North, which is home to the world's 130,000 Eskimos, it is cold most of the year. Only the months of June, July, and August have temperatures that average above freezing. The rest of the time it is bitterly cold, with temperatures sometimes reaching –70 degrees Fahrenheit. In the deepest part of winter the sun disappears entirely for months at a time. And because the territory inhabited by the Eskimos is far above the timberline—too far north for trees to grow—the frigid arctic winds blow unchecked over the ice, making the darkness and cold that much more unfriendly. It is no wonder that the first explorers to visit these northern places called them "the barrens," for it seemed that nothing could survive here.

But ever since the Eskimo people migrated across the ice from northern Asia to Alaska and Canada thousands of years ago, they have survived. In a climate with no forests or prairies filled with game, Eskimos learned to hunt whales, seals, and snow birds. In a treeless region where lumber for construction was not available, Eskimos learned how to build homes with snow and sod. And in a land that provided no easy supply of fuel, Eskimos learned how to use the oil from seals and whales to sustain the fires that heated their dwellings.

## The Real People

One thing the Eskimos did not have to contend with was war. While to the south, many Native American nations were battling over land and hunting territories, no one wished to challenge the Eskimos over the ice and snow of their homelands. The two Native American nations that lived closest to the Eskimos were the Naskapi and the Cree, and neither ventured north of the timberline.[1] It was they, in fact, who first gave these northern people the name "Eskimantsies," which means "eaters of raw meat."

The people of the Far North called themselves Inuit, Inupiat, or Yupik, which all mean, in various dialects,[2] "the Real People." (This [reading] uses "Eskimo," for today this term may refer to northern people who live in either Alaska or Canada.)

Through the centuries Eskimos have existed on their own, with very little influence from outside their world. Even while explorers from Europe, busy investigating the lands to the south, had begun pushing Native Americans farther and farther west, the Eskimos'

---

1. **timberline** line above which trees do not grow
2. **dialects** forms of language spoken in a specific region, community, or social group

world remained untouched. Strengthened by their close-knit families, the Real People needed no more than keen eyes and steady aims to hunt for food, and the wisdom of their elders to guide them.

## "They Laugh at Us"

But although Eskimos were left alone longer than native people to the south, the outside world eventually crept in. And as more and more outsiders came to the Far North, they saw that the Arctic was not as barren and useless as most people had believed. The Eskimos' lands were a valuable source of great wealth—at first from whaling ships, then from fur traders, and more recently from traffickers in gold and oil.

Life in Eskimo villages has drastically changed with increased contact from outsiders, especially in the past fifty years—and some maintain that that change has been for the better. Technology never before available to the Eskimo people is now commonplace in northern villages. Powerful motorboats have largely replaced the traditional kayaks and umiaks, the precisely engineered, skincovered boats used for hunting. It's much more common to see a sleek, modern snowmobile than a team of sled dogs outside the home of an Eskimo hunter. Modern medicine can cure Eskimo children of diseases that only a few generations ago would have killed them. Once a culture that was on the move, following the migratory patterns of the animals on which they depended, the Eskimos now live in permanent villages. Famine and mass starvation are a thing of the past.

But many feel that Eskimos in Alaska and the Canadian Arctic lost more than they gained by their new relationship with the outside world. Few hunt to feed their families; instead, people rely on canned and frozen food from village grocery stores. As a result, many of the skills that used to be handed down from generation to generation are being lost. Alcoholism is epidemic; the use of drugs like cocaine and crack is growing among the young people. And the stories and songs of the elders are taking a backseat to video games.

Many Eskimos worry about the future of their culture. Exposure via[3] television to the material culture of the United States and Canada has made many young Eskimos embarrassed and ashamed of their lifestyle. "The world thinks we live in snow igloos and chew

---

3. **via** by means of

cold whale meat or something," says an Inuit teen. "They laugh at us. Those kids [in Canada and the United States] don't think we're like them at all, but we are."

Many young Inuit agree. It's hard, they say, for those who live outside their world to understand them. And how could they, wonders one Inuit girl, when the Eskimo world is so remote that it is almost invisible to outsiders? The world map used to show weather patterns and world events doesn't even show the Arctic homeland of the Real People. "I live in those two inches above the television screen," this perceptive teenager laughs. "I live in the two inches of Canada that you can't see."

## Between Two Skins

In the Inuit language, the word *aqunnaaki*, which means, literally, "between two skins," is used to refer to teenagers. They are neither grownups nor children—they are in two separate worlds, not at home in either one. Those who have taken time to learn about the Eskimos say that in many ways, *all* Eskimos are *aqunnaaki*—they are between the "skins" of the old, familiar culture of their elders and the new modern way of life.

Charlotte and
David Yue

from

# The Igloo

*The demands of the Arctic climate and Alaska's location give Alaskans a different perspective from people who live in the other forty-nine states.*

## Living in an Igloo

### Food

Eskimos lived healthy lives on a diet that consisted almost entirely of meat and fish. They hunted whatever animals were most readily available at that particular season, and no source of meat was overlooked. Although boiled meat was preferred when there was enough fuel, some meat was eaten uncooked. Raw meat gives more energy and nourishment than the same amount of cooked meat. Often Eskimos enjoyed cooked food at the end of the day when they were going to rest after the meal, but ate raw meat while they were active outdoors hunting or traveling.

Eskimos also ate internal organs and animal skins that were not considered edible[1] by the Europeans who came to the Arctic. These people were often horrified by Eskimo eating habits, but many who refused to eat Eskimo food became very sick and some died. Travelers in the Arctic mostly suffered from scurvy, a disease caused by vitamin C deficiency.[2] Internal organs and fresh meat are rich in vitamins. White men who ate an Eskimo diet learned that it could prevent and cure scurvy.

Eskimos would not eat polar bear livers. They believed these should be offered in gratitude for successful hunting and to honor the

---

1. **edible** fit to be eaten
2. **deficiency** shortage; lack

spirit of the animal killed. Many explorers who did not trust Eskimo wisdom became sick. Modern research has shown that the polar bear's liver can be very poisonous, containing harmful levels of vitamin A.

Eskimos ate a large quantity of meat in times of plenty—four to eight pounds a day. In cold weather and especially when they were traveling, one half of their food was fat. Having to live mainly on lean meat was the same as starving to Eskimos, no matter how large a quantity of lean meat was available. A steady diet of lean meat could cause serious illness or death.

Food was usually cooked by boiling. The large rectangular kettle was placed over the lamp on a four-legged frame or was supported above the lamp by a horizontal pole. Snow or ice was melted in the pot and available food was added to be simmered into a rich stew.

There is very little edible plant life in the Arctic. Berries and wild plants were gathered when available—bilberries, black crowberries, cloudberries, willow leaves, mountain sorrel leaves, and some roots. These were eaten fresh, mixed with blubber,[3] added to the cooking pot to be boiled with the rest of the meal, or stored for later use. Studies have shown that the plants preferred by nearly all native groups were those with the highest content of important vitamins, and that Eskimo methods of storing and preparing them were excellent for preserving their nutritional value. The white people living in the Arctic generally preferred different species, which we have learned were of less nutritional value. Although plants accounted for only a small quantity of the Eskimo diet, they did provide important vitamins and nutrients. They were a regular part of Eskimo meals when available, and they were considered important enough to be gathered every year. Over the years Eskimos had learned by trial and error which foods were healthful for them.

## Families

In the Arctic, with its limited resources, a family was very much on its own. When there was not enough food available to support large numbers of people, families went their separate ways, surviving as best they could. When they formed larger communities, these were really a collection of families. Each family member was important and had specific jobs to do. Families cared deeply about each other, but

---

3. **blubber** fat from whales or other sea mammals

the welfare of the family as a whole was the most important consideration.

Fathers were highly respected. The life of everyone in the family depended on his hunting skills for food. It was a source of great pride and satisfaction for a man to be known as a good provider for his family, the elderly, and neighbors who were in need. Men were also responsible for transportation. They took care of the sledge[4] and the dog team and made and used the kayak.[5] They made weapons, tools, and utensils, including things used by women. Men built the igloos and put up the tents.

The mother was the center of the family, always busy taking care of the home, preparing food, tending the oil lamp night and day, caring for and playing with the children. She sewed and mended the clothing, bedding, tents, and boat coverings. She did some hunting and fishing and collected plants, berries, and eggs. She was loved and needed.

Children spent their first years close to their mothers, carried against their backs, secure in being loved, cared for, and highly valued. Young children had few responsibilities, but their play often helped them learn skills they would need later on. Boys made hunting implements[6] and used snow sculptures for target practice. Later they practiced hunting small animals. They also sometimes built small playhouses. Girls had dolls or puppies to play with and often sewed small clothing and shoes for their dolls. Often young children were not even required to help carry a pack when traveling. During the times of continuous daylight, children would play outside far into the night hours. As they grew older, they participated in family activities by helping their parents. If children were orphaned, they were adopted by relatives or by a childless family and were accepted as part of that family.

Men and women were rarely idle[7] at home. There was always mending to be done or new things to be made. Visitors often brought their work and kept busy while they chatted. Work was carefully done and many utensils were very beautiful.

---

4. **sledge**  sled or sleigh used for carrying loads
5. **kayak**  one-person canoe
6. **implements**  tools
7. **idle**  inactive; not busy

Families were very close and each member depended on the others. Although jobs were separated, there were many times when [family members] needed to help each other. Women helped with hunting and housebuilding when they were needed. If a woman was very busy with sewing, her husband would help. Survival depended on families working together.

Eskimos believed in a spirit world. Animals, hills, streams, and all things in nature had souls. Angry spirits could cause hard times. Being killed by a crudely[8] made weapon might offend[9] an animal's spirit, which would warn his brother animals of the hunter's disrespect. When a seal was killed, the hunter's wife poured fresh water in the seal's mouth, hoping that its soul would tell other seals and that they would want to be caught for the chance to drink fresh, clear water. When the family moved out of a tent or house, they lifted the back of the tent or broke through the back of the snowhouse. They believed that by doing this they could trick any bad spirit trying to follow them to their new house.

## Games and Pastimes

Igloos usually rang with laughter and fun. It was especially important to have ways of passing the time during the long weeks of darkness. During the dark days time passed slowly. Storms and blizzards put a stop to all hunting, and often it was not safe to venture outdoors at all. Eskimos ate and slept, talked and told stories, and danced and played games.

In the summer, when the sun shone all night long, people did not feel like sleeping and games continued happily. Children played make-believe. Boys had toy sledges, bows and arrows, kayaks, and harpoons. Girls played with dolls of ivory, wood, or caribou skin stuffed with hair. They had small lamps, *ulus*,[10] cooking utensils, and cooking pots. Fathers carved small ice toys for their children. Children spent a lot of time playing outside. Girls sometimes had story knives, which they used to draw pictures in the snow illustrating the story they were telling. They could smooth over one picture and draw the next.

---

8. **crudely** not carefully; roughly
9. **offend** displease; insult; anger
10. *ulus* multi-purpose tools; knives with semicircular blades and wooden or bone handles

There were many games for grown-ups as well as children. In one game they tried to catch a piece of bone with holes in it on a stick. The bone was attached to the stick by a cord. Different holes had different values. In another game a piece of bone with holes in it was hung from the roof. At the signal all players would strike at the holes with a stick. The winner was the one who got his stick in the hole. Sometimes a knife was laid on the platform and spun around. The person the knife pointed at would have to perform a task set by the others. Eskimos played different kinds of gambling games. They also liked competitive games—wrestling, tug-of-war, jumping over ropes, and ball games. Cat's cradle was a favorite Eskimo game, and they made complex string figures representing animals, hunters, spirits, and familiar things in their lives. Dancing was one of their greatest pleasures. There were masked dances and dances performed with a drum. Dances frequently brightened the long, dark winter days.

## Snow Villages

### Settlements

Eskimos lived a roaming life, but they followed a pattern in their movements. Groups had places to which they returned every year and formed settlements for larger, cooperative hunting ventures.[11] People got together to socialize and trade and for ceremonies and dances. For the Central Eskimos, summer settlements were groups of tents; winter villages were clusters of snow huts.

In winter villages, connected igloos were sometimes built to be shared by several families. These would have two or more snowhouses, storage rooms, and a dog shelter[, all] with one common exit. People could go from house to house and room to room without going outside. Large igloos housing more than one family often had two platforms. These could connect with smaller houses in one snow block.

There was often a large dance house in the village that served as a meeting place for singing, dancing, feasting, and ceremonies. Sometimes two large connected snowhouses were built with platforms, one for the men and one for the women. Dances were performed under the arch joining the two houses. In some areas the

---

11. **ventures** risky or dangerous undertakings

festivals or dances were held in one large igloo. This usually had no platform; men stood on one side and women on the other. The lamp was on a block of snow in the middle. Several family dwellings might be built around the large meeting chamber . . .

Many of the activities in the dance house were held for the enjoyment of socializing with friends. People got together for informal singing, dancing, contests, and fun. Sometimes dancers wore comic masks and held contests, trying to make each other laugh. A storyteller would promise to tell a story no one had ever heard to the end and stretch the tale out until his audience had fallen asleep.

The dance house was also a place for artistic performances. Eskimos lived in an environment where life was a constant struggle to meet basic needs, but art was one of those needs. Creating beautiful tools, utensils, and clothing was important. Their music, dancing, singing, and storytelling also filled a creative need. Some of the dances had fixed motions that were rehearsed and carefully performed. Other songs and dances were improvised[12] for a particular occasion. The stories and legends spun by storytellers to fill the endless winter nights formed the oral tradition passed on from generation to generation. A good story or song eventually spread from one village to another throughout the Arctic.

The plan of a settlement varied every time it was built. When families rebuilt igloos at another site or when they reassembled the next season, they built houses that were as simple or as elaborate as they needed at that particular time.

## Community Life

Eskimos thought of themselves as part of a village. Villages had traditional territories where they hunted. They varied in size from about thirty to five hundred people. The settlement needed enough people for hunting ventures that required cooperation, and enough people to survive disasters. But the land could not support too large a community. A number of these villages dotted the shores about ten to thirty miles apart. Visiting, trading, and socializing among villages was fairly frequent.

Large settlements united people who had been separated for a long time. There were always stories and gossip to be shared when the

---

12. **improvised** made up on the spur of the moment, without preparation

people got together. Women were in and out of each other's igloos during the day. The whole community came out to greet the hunters on their return, to see how successful they had been and to hear the accounts of the hunt.

In the igloo, hunters told of their deeds, acting out the dangers and how they had faced them. In addition to providing lively conversation, gatherings where people could tell the stories of their hunting experiences were good places for sharing information. Eskimos always wanted to learn as much as they could, and they listened carefully as their fellow hunters told of their experiences. Hunters shared information they had heard from other people as well as their own personal observations. The body of knowledge of the group was always being enlarged and improved in this way. Eskimos were always able to find humor in mistakes and misfortunes. Things often went wrong, and Eskimos knew that anger never helped. Hunters never tired of recounting their most frustrating errors and laughing about them with their friends.

Sharing was an important part of survival in the Arctic. Eskimos worked out meat-sharing arrangements so that everyone got a fair share of food. Each hunter had a partner for sharing a particular part of the animal. The hunter always gave the seal's flipper to his flipper-partner, who would do the same when he had a successful hunt. Partners were appointed at the time of a young man's first kill. Giving gifts of food to widows, elderly, or needy people brought good luck to the hunter. Eskimos were willing to share what they had with someone who was not a good hunter as long as they did not think he was lazy.

Each family in the village made what it needed. Individuals might become known as experts in a certain technique—best knife maker, fastest seamstress, or most skillful walrus hunter. But people did not specialize in one particular activity. Everyone needed to be versatile and able to do many jobs.

There was no formal government in these villages. They did not have chiefs or councils to regulate activities. Leaders of hunting parties were chosen because they had skills and abilities that were needed at the time. The leaders rarely gave orders and always consulted the other hunters. Individuals who were respected for their wisdom might be called on for help and advice in community matters.

A shaman[13] was perhaps the most influential person in the community. He was believed to have supernatural powers and was often more feared than respected. People consulted shamans to find out when bad weather would stop, where lost articles could be found, when animals were best hunted, or when strangers would come. The shaman would evoke[14] spirits to cure sickness, give strength to a hunter, or help the community. People also came to shamans when they were angry at someone and wanted revenge.

Eskimos had many taboos, things that were forbidden because they were believed to be dangerous. Many of these restrictions were made by the shamans. Some were handed down for generations and applied to all people; others applied only to a particular situation. A sick person might not be allowed to eat certain foods just because the shaman ordered it, not for any medical reasons. Taboos were enforced by threats of bad luck or sickness.

One of the most important spirits to Eskimos was Sedna. She lived at the bottom of the sea and controlled the sea animals. When she was angry, she sent storms or kept the seals and walruses with her. When animals became scarce, the shaman would go into a trance. He would communicate with Sedna to find out what had angered her and what the people must do to make her release the animals again.

Daily life in the Arctic was full of dangers. Eskimos faced many hardships that were beyond their control. Many people carved ivory figures to carry with them for luck in hunting. Any charms or ceremonies that might bring good luck were useful and important to them. Villagers held dances and ceremonies in the large dance house to honor the spirits of the animals they hunted.

## Traveling in the Arctic

### How Eskimos Found Their Way

Eskimos were always studying the secrets of their environment and of the animals that lived in it. Their knowledge and understanding was handed down and expanded by generations of hunters. Eskimos noticed small changes in the color of ice, in patches of snow, and in the texture of water, and they studied the meanings of these

---

13. **shaman** priest believed to have magical powers to cure illness
14. **evoke** call on; summon

tiny clues. But the signals given by the land could suddenly be obscured by fog, snow, rain, wind, glare, or darkness. Even short journeys could become perilous.[15] Travel was a part of the Eskimos life. Men made regular excursions in search of food. Eskimo often traveled great distances—as much as two hundred miles. Small groups sometimes traveled together or an individual would go alone. They were skillful travelers.

When making a long journey to an unfamiliar area, the traveler would try to find someone who knew the country and could draw a map. Eskimos observed the landscape very carefully, took notice of all the details, and could draw very accurate maps on pieces of dried gut. They told directions from the sun, stars, or prevailing winds. Wind blew the snow into rows of snow mounds. They marked directions as they followed or crossed these rows. They measured distances by "sleepings," the number of times they stopped to sleep. Time could not easily be measured by the sun in the Arctic.

Sometimes they marked routes by setting stones on end at prominent points. Sledge routes that offered the best terrain for travel could sometimes be used as trails by other hunters—but travel conditions changed abruptly.

Eskimos seldom turned back once they set out on a journey, regardless of the difficulties they faced. But they were wise enough not to begin traveling if they thought there was danger involved. They refused to travel in any kind of weather in which they could easily lose their way.

Every hunter needed to understand the behavior of animals, but it was equally important to understand the behavior of ice. Eskimos studied every move and change in the ice. They judged the safety of ice by its color. Water shows through thin, clear ice making it appear very dark; as it thickens, it becomes gray. Hunters knew that even gray ice was not uniform.[16] There were always patches of thin ice, and they needed to watch the ice carefully to guide their dog teams safely. Holes, cracks, and areas of weak ice were easily hidden by drifting snow.

Eskimos were always looking for signs of game whenever they traveled, but they still kept alert for unexpected situations, changes in

---

15. **perilous** dangerous
16. **uniform** all the same

their surroundings, or indications of changing weather conditions. Eskimos noticed that stars twinkled and danced noticeably a day or two before a storm wind. During calm, clear weather stars do not twinkle as much. Warmer weather often preceded[17] a storm and temperatures often dropped near the end of a storm.

Every hunter's knowledge went beyond what was essential for ordinary travel and hunting. He also had a large store of information that he could call on in emergency situations. Eskimos learned the best way to walk on thin ice by observing polar bears. A man would spread his legs as wide as possible and slide his feet quickly along the ice. If he still could not make it to safe ice, he would lie flat and squirm along with arms and legs stretched out. No Eskimos would ever give a demonstration of the technique on thin ice to show off his skill or even to teach someone else. Eskimos could not understand people doing dangerous things for excitement or competition. Eskimos never took unnecessary risks.

Eskimo hunters and travelers had to be creative and imaginative. They frequently needed these skills to make or repair equipment along their way. When they faced a problem, they devised[18] a solution. Eskimos rarely gave up a task until it was completed, and they realized that jobs not done well caused more work in the long run. A hunter tried to use as little energy as possible and always looked for shortcuts. Energy was a valuable commodity.[19] Eskimos often traveled a greater distance to follow the smoothest trail and avoid rough places. In the long run this used much less energy.

---

17. **preceded**  happened before
18. **devised**  invented
19. **commodity**  resource; basic item